Marty Bartlett is a [illegible] fishermen fishing from Florida to Maine longlining for large pelagics and groundfish. He now proves to us he is a also a fine author. A well written commercial fishing novel is a great thing. Thank you, Marty.

—Captain Mathew Thomson, F/V *Saretta*, Monhegan, Maine

It's refreshing to read a book about commercial fishing written by someone with the knowledge and experience Marty has. You get a real feel for what these fishermen's lives were like at a time when there were still large stocks of fish but little of the technology that has so depleted them.

Marty has been a successful fisherman and storyteller for a long time and has combined the two into a book I didn't want to put down.

—Matt Samuels, F/V *Mamosa*, Rockport, Maine

Fishermen fish and writers write, but rarely do you find someone who does both as well as Marty Bartlett. His novel, built around the experiences of a young excoastguardsman on his first trip as a commercial fisherman, tells a good story made better by the enormous amount of information about fish and fishing that he weaves into it. Anyone who has watched a fishing boat bound for sea and wondered what life is like for the men and women who man her will find the answer in *Wind Shift at Peaked Hills*.

—George Cadwalader, F/V *Frannie Cahoon*, Woods Hole, MA
Founder of the Penikese Island school and author of
Castaways: *The Penikese Island Experiment*, and
The Unmarked Road

Wind Shift at Peaked Hills

Martin R. Bartlett

Wind Shift at Peaked Hills

By Martin R. Bartlett

Cover art by W. Goadby Lawrence

Book design by Tim Seymour

This account is a work of fiction.

If any of the characters resemble people living or dead

it is purely coincidental.

In Memoriam

Juliette W. Edge

John Bell

Steven Giese

Seth A. Carey

Ronnie K. Stires

Frank F. Carey

Dave Masch

Doug Swihart

Fine Fishers...Fine Friends

To Whom this book is dedicated

Acknowledgments

I would like to thank Kay and Dana Gibson for recycling their Wang computer in my direction. This work was started as a result of their generosity.

Jeff and Deb Kaufmann kindly made my Wang work fit for Apple consumption.

Susan Pollack, Robert Hill, Rebecca Bartlett, Franklin Reeve, George Cadwalader, Dana and Kay Gibson read parts of the text and provided helpful suggestions and encouragement.

My prep school classmate Tad Harvey spent countless hours of his valuable time walking me through high school English that I neglected while hatching schemes to sample the headmaster's stocked trout pond. I am forever indebted to this most kind and talented friend.

Joanne Ricca provided the final polish and Tim Seymour the artistry and expertise to put it all together.

Thank you one and all.
MRB

Introduction

In the beginning, the outer Cape was a ragged forty-mile long pile of sand, clay, and boulders bulldozed together by two lobes of glacier. As many tons of ice melted and the sea level rose, wind, waves and tidal currents smoothed the random relief of this obstacle and created graceful peninsulas on the northern and southern extremities. Shaped like fishermen's gaff hooks, these promontories provided choice sanctuaries for shoals of fish. Early settlers quickly established communities that subsisted on these abundant resources and traded them far and wide. Eventually the stocks were diminished, and the sanctuaries became shelters for fleets of larger and larger craft required to go farther and farther offshore to catch the same fish that had once been caught within sight of the beach.

In a poignant reminder of how over-fishing contributes to the hazards of an already risky occupation, fishermen joined explorers and merchantmen running bars and clawing off lee shores. The spit of sand extending from the south end of Cape Cod's outer beach was quickly labeled "Malabar." The northern promontory, known as the Province Lands, is bordered by a shoal named Peaked Hill Bars. Oriented east and west, a few hundred yards off a beach recognized by a series of tall sand dunes, Peaked Hill Bars are perfectly positioned to hammer mariners lured toward the shelter of Provincetown harbor. Riding an approaching storm's preliminary northeaster, vessels that are passed by the center of the storm experience a wind shift to the northwest that can force them onto the shoals to leeward, instead of into the harbor of refuge a few miles away.

The following is an account of a longline fishing trip to Georges Bank that succeeds in avoiding Peaked Hill Bars, but not all of the distress that accompanies this romantic calling. It takes place at a time before the use of monofilament nylon mainline, chemical light attractors, and radio transmitter buoys. It takes place at a time when these refinements were not necessary.

Author's Note

Historical timelines have been contracted to prolong the existence of the breeches buoy in the Coast Guard and include southern competition into the narrative.

Table of Contents

Wind Shift at Peaked Hills

The Province Lands

Viewed from a distance it could have been a biblical pilgrimage through the wilderness, a line of dark figures plodding through a black and gray landscape of weathered scrub vegetation under a leaden sky. Days of rain had released the pungent aroma of decaying foliage from sun-baked beach plum and bayberry that had somehow eked nourishment from the sandy soil. A streak of brightening sky over the Black Hills in the western bay promised a windshift and clearing. But not even the wildly wagging tail on the ample black butt of his canine companion, disappearing under a clump of scrub pine, could raise Leonard Hill's spirits as he trudged along. He already hated this place. He had hated it ever since the scalloper *Polly Eldridge* had died on the outer bar four years earlier. The smell of the place reminded him of the sweat of beaten men, the rain, the tears of their women.

Peaked Hills Lifeboat Station

It had been Hill's first assignment after boot camp. He'd been sent to a remote lifeboat station called Peaked Hills on the northern tip of Cape Cod. He soon discovered why the hills of sand were peaked. For nine months a year when the wind wasn't screeching from the northeast, it was screeching from the northwest. Small tufts of beach grass topped each hill, giving it a jaunty look, belying the grasses' ultimate effect: to gather more sand.

After six months, Leonard was getting used to the isolation, the boredom of watches, the repetitive cleaning and the chicken-shit inspections. He even got used to the crusty white-haired chief boatswain who followed him around, finding "holidays" in Hill's washing of sandblasted windows that were too frosted to see through. There were breaks in the monotony. Every Saturday, in good weather, the station invited the public to the weekly breeches buoy and lifeboat drills to practice the crew's lifesaving skills and familiarize the public with rescue methods and equipment. Lenny would watch, entranced, as the boatswain's mate spooned black powder into little red cloth bags. "One and two and one to be good on," the mate recited. Hill loved the deep throaty report of this sturdy little brass howitzer, the cloud of white smoke, the smell of burned black powder and the beautiful arc of the messenger line following the 18-pound projectile through the upright arms of the practice mast behind the station. He'd never forget the squealing tail block as the breeches buoy came down the hawser from the practice mast with some grinning local kid in it who came to the station each Saturday to be "saved." The breeches buoy was a pair of canvas pants sewn to a cork life ring hung on a four-part bridle. The tail block was a pulley hauled to a vessel by the messenger line. Through the tail block rove the whip line that delivered the hawser from which the breeches buoy would be suspended with a snatch block. The whip line would subsequently pull the snatch and buoy back and forth between the stranded vessel and the beach.

After one drill Lenny asked the mate if he could overhaul the block and put some grease on the pin. The mate told him to figure out why this wasn't such a good idea. Finally relenting, he explained to the stymied Hill that sand washing into a greased pulley on the way through the surf would not wash out before it was hauled aboard a stricken vessel. A dry bearing was better than one clogged with a slurry of sand and grease.

Lifeboat drills were the sole escape from oppressive shore-side supervision. Vaulting over the fair weather surf with short choppy strokes, the four-man crew would settle into a slower cruising stroke making for the closest dragger in hopes of bumming a six-pack. Leonard especially enjoyed this exercise when the chief boatswain, due for weekend liberty, would wildly gesticulate for their return from the top of a sand dune while they rested on their oars and enjoyed their beers behind convenient offshore swells. Leaning on his steering oar, the coxswain would parody boot camp rowing commands, timing orders like "Stand by to guzzle," at the top of a wave and "Quaff a quickie" in the trough between waves. With the onset of the hurricane season, a sense of foreboding replaced the cheap thrills of summer. Spectators disappeared and Saturday drills lost their festive atmosphere. The surf was often too high for the chief to risk launching a boat. But it was the night the *Polly* came ashore that sealed Lenny's hatred for this God-forsaken place.

The Grounding

Big storms always give plenty of warning. But the warning comes in a whisper called a "weather breeder" — a glassy calm day or two when distant shores seem twice their normal height, sound travels long distances, and smoke hugs the horizon. It is a signal, not unlike the tapping of a conductor's baton on his lectern, silencing divergent individual whimpering, preparing the listener for a powerful cooperative event.

Stan Eldridge had known there was snotty weather coming. For three days he had feverishly worked a small but thick bed of scallops four miles east of Chatham. It was the kind of fishing he loved. His three-man crew never got a break. After the first dredge hit the deck they never caught up with the pile of uncut shellfish. He promised them a kink if they cleared the deck before the next tow came aboard. Though they worked steadily, the pile of scallops just kept getting bigger. After three days they had a hundred eighty forty-pound bags below and a load on deck that prohibited further fishing. The exhausted crew fell into their bunks. Stan put a freshening southwester on the *Polly*'s tail and headed for the anchorage at Provincetown. There his refreshed gang could whittle away on the deck load of shell stock during the spell of inclement weather ahead.

Eldridge hugged the coast to avoid the combers generated by the ebbing tidal current farther offshore. By dusk he had left Nauset Light's three flashes behind. The wind had backed into the southeast, but he was only a few miles from Highland Light where he could once more put the wind on his tail. He was dead tired and kept blacking out. He opened the leeward pilothouse door, turned the radio up and the autopilot off. He'd be inside by midnight. All he needed was to keep his head clear and his blood circulating.

What Stan Eldridge was too tired to comprehend was that the deepening gale he rode north was overtaking him at a forward speed of 40 knots, five times faster than the eight he was making good. Its closest point of approach would occur two hours after he passed Highland Light. Just after he had hoped to put the wind on his tail for the last time, it would come shrieking down from the northwest as the center of the storm moved on toward Nova Scotia.

There are times at half tide when the slope of the beach is at just the right angle so that waves surging up the incline will return offshore with force enough to result in "angel wings" on the bar when they meet shore-bound breakers. A less beautiful and more dangerous version of this phenomenon occurs when seas coming from the same direction wrap around an obstacle and meet in what one might suppose to be a shelter. Seamen seeking safety in such a lee will instead find a place where every third wave is a rogue wave : two ordinary waves one on the shoulders of the another. That night the Polly was approaching Peaked Hill Bars at 10:30 when a white-topped wall of black picked her up and laid her on her port beam. A ton of dredges landed on top of a deck load of scallops that had slid up against scuppers, closed to keep the shellfish aboard. Stan Eldridge found himself dangling from the wheel, his feet in the water that now lapped at the sill of the open pilothouse door. The *Polly* tried to recover. She came back to a 40-degree angle before the next wave rolled her back to 60 degrees.

Eldridge got his feet on the doorframe and pulled the wheel full to port. Then he climbed up on the wheel so he could reach the throttle lever, jamming it as far forward as it would go in an attempt to right the *Polly*. But every time she started to turn, another sea would pick her up and return her to the trough. Eldridge had to try to get the dredges off the scallops and open the scuppers. He clambered over the bridge wing railing, jumped to the winch and pulled himself forward hand over hand on the towing wire, to the starboard gallows. He shouted instructions to the pale faces that greeted him from the forecastle doghouse. Scrambling back to the winches, he got them in gear and jerked the starboard dredge off the scallops and up to the gallows where it slammed against the rail.

Eldridge was about to hoist the port dredge when the *Polly* hit the bar. The sickening thud shook the rigging. Feeling his stomach turn, Eldridge scrambled back to the pilothouse yelling to the crew to get into their life jackets. Grabbing the radio mike, he switched from the weather channel to the calling and distress frequency. In as calm a voice as he could manage he called, "Coast Guard, Coast Guard, this is the fishing vessel *Polly Eldridge*, the *Polly Eldridge*. We are aground on Peaked Hill…" He continued with the Loran numbers and the number of people aboard but in the middle of his transmission there was another jarring thud and a cracking sound.

In the watchtower at his station, the last word Leonard Hill heard was "Peaked." He was calling Race Point station to confirm what he had heard when Boston District radio walked over a reply: "Peaked Hill this is Nan Mike Fox One. You have a stranding. Deploy your equipment. Keep this unit informed of your progress." Hill opened a lee window. Sure enough, there was a loom of white haze offshore of a dune two miles east of the station.

Hill joined the group of men struggling into foul weather gear as they made their way toward the lights coming from an open bay of the garage. Through sheets of rain, he could make out the tractor's headlights shining through a cloud of exhaust. Over the howling wind, he could hear the chatter of a cold engine operating on less than its full complement of cylinders. In spite of some shelter in the lee of the tractor and beach cart, a slurry of sand and fluffy yellow spume showered them as they trudged through the dunes. By the time they reached a break in the dunes opposite the Polly, they were bathed in sweat. The chief boatswain was shaking his head as they set up the breeches buoy. It was going to be a long shot. He lay on his belly to sight the gun, tinkering nervously with the elevation wedge that would determine the trajectory of the projectile. Finally, stepping back, he barked, "Stand clear-ready-fire" as he jerked the firing lanyard with a savage flourish of his arm. Lenny couldn't believe this was the same cannon that sounded so powerful during drills behind the station. The gale made a sizable belly in the messenger line that must have snubbed the projectile's progress, because there was no tell-tale taking up of slack by the crew of the *Polly* that would indicate a successful shot.

Knowing the mate's propensity for spiking powderbags, the boatswain told him to have the next try while he sought the shelter of the beach cart to light a cigarette. The mate tied another messenger to a new projectile. Hill watched with awe as he stuffed four red bags of powder down the barrel of the brass cannon. The "Action at Wrecks" section of Instruction for Coast Guard Stations clearly states that "the standard charge of powder for the Lyle gun in practice or drill with the beach apparatus is 2 ounces." And farther, "The maximum charge of 6 ounces shall not be exceeded except under extraordinary circumstances, but in no case more than 8 ounces, may be used." The mate had just loaded 12 ounces of powder into the little cannon. Replacing the spent ignition blank, he shoved the elevation wedge in a step to bring the muzzle down. Then crouching, he moved as far away as the lanyard would allow. He didn't have to warn the crew, who had been closely watching him. They scurried for the safety of the tractor and beach cart as he raised his fist with the lanyard in a gesture of defiance. There was a tongue of orange flame, a mighty report, and a cloud of white smoke. Over the gale and his ringing ears, the mate heard an expletive come from behind the beach cart followed by the appearance of chief boatswain's red face. The Lyle gun lay on its back, dug muzzle first into the sand, eight feet behind the firing line. The messenger line still snaked out of the faking box. From over the roar of the surf, a sharp cracking sound reached the beach as the messenger projectile passed through the bottom of a Banks dory in its cradle over the starboard wing of the *Polly*'s pilothouse.

Ashore, the messenger, made fast to the tail block and whip lines, disappeared into the surf. The desperate crew of the *Polly* made quick work of fastening the tail block and the hawser line that followed to the mainmast, but no matter how the lifesavers ashore hauled, they could not raise the hawser high enough to clear the raging surf. They would have to haul the breeches buoy off to the *Polly* through the surf and hope for the best.

On the first haul they dragged the beaten body of Eldridge's son from the breeches. The second haul came ashore empty. Before they completed hauling the buoy offshore a third time the hawser went slack. The sweet smell of scallops reached the beach before they had completely retrieved the hawser at the end of which was the mainmast of the *Polly Eldridge.*

They had left the breeches buoy apparatus where it lay, the bags of scallops where they beached. The beach cart bore the bodies of the *Polly*'s crew back thru the dunes to the station. It was well after midnight when they arrived. The crowd that awaited them included Stan Eldridge's wife and daughter.

District headquarters offered the station crew transfers to units of their choice. At first they all declined. But then, one by one, the haunting memory and sleepless nights wore them down. Requests for sea duty appeared on the chief boatswain's desk. In six months they had all been replaced.

Ashes to Ashes

As Hill brought up the rear in the trail of silent mourners, he was reminded once again that he was here because he had volunteered. When the folks ahead of him, wading through the wet sand in street shoes, began to complain, he recalled the mate stuffing four bags of powder into the Lyle gun, and slogged toward the head of the procession. Overtaking the leader as they arrived together at the top of a rise, he held a free elbow as the rest of the group gathered just shy of the summit. Wordlessly, a female figure half turned and with eyes closed, held a cobalt blue urn at arm's length. Painfully, reluctantly, the urn tipped and Hill watched in wonder as the black and gray contents disappeared into the black and gray landscape on the eddies of the southwest wind.

Lenny had seen calm days at sea when the water and sky were indistinguishable. Calm nights on bow watch when the stars shone at him from 360 degrees. He had seen rough days offshore when by their contortions, the wind and sea seemed hell-bent on becoming one. But he had never seen a man's remains disappear in the wind between the clouds and a piece of land he had come to dread. Slowly, reluctantly, he felt the hatred draining out of him; falling on the sand with a few stubborn black particles from the urn. Soon it would be replaced with despair that would eventually become thankfulness as he weighed the events that had brought him back to this place he hadn't revisited in four years.

THE SAILOR'S CONSOLATION. Stanza I

One night came on a hurricane,
The sea was mountains rolling,
When Barney Buntline turned his quid
And said to Billy Bowling:
"A strong northwester's blowing, Bill;
Hark! Don't ye hear it roar, now?
Lord help'em, how I pities all
Unhappy folks on shore now!"
William Pitt [?-1840]

Woods Hole

Lenny Hill was bustin' rust. He sat on a milk crate swinging hammers from both gloved hands, knocking welts of rust off the steel bulkhead with a diamond-shaped chipping hammer, going after deep pits with the pointed end of a welding hammer. Coming to large slabs of rust, he picked up the 12-ounce ball peen lying on deck between his feet and belted the surface until the brittle scale flew free from the more resilient good steel beneath. A pair of engine-room ear guards protected him from the rhythmic tattoo, a pair of plastic goggles deflected the flying rust particles from his eyes. He hummed a reggae tune, half hypnotized in his insulated world. Concentrating on the syncopated rapping of the hammers, he didn't notice the young woman's approach until she tapped him on the shoulder.

"Buy you a beer if you back off that bullshit for half an hour," she drawled beseechingly. Lenny paused, half turning, to see denim disappear down the forecastle doghouse.

"Breakfast of champions," he thought, removing his gloves and headgear.

A large Styrofoam cup of regular coffee and a glazed donut sat on a paper towel at one corner of the galley table. The coffee girl, with her nose buried in another cup, sat at another corner staring at a dog-eared copy of *Mademoiselle*. Lenny sat down and took a tentative sip of the hot liquid. The girl came up for air, glanced at him and smiled.

"You must be Lenny Hill," she said, looking back at the magazine. She had straight black hair pulled back in a braid, watery blue eyes that danced, thin lips that seemed to reach from ear to ear and a pug nose that might have been pressed on with someone's thumb.

"And you must be Franny Miller," he offered, wondering if she could touch her nose with her tongue.

"You got it," she said, slowly turning a page, preoccupied, guzzling another life and death swallow of coffee. Her wrinkled chambray shirt was buttoned to the waist where the tails were tied. Her build was slight, wiry and taut. Her ringless hands, small and powerful, remained curled when at rest like the talons of a raptor. Calluses were well defined by indelible discoloration that identified the nature of the owner's occupation as fingerprints identify an individual.

"I've got to stow some grub and clean the stove this afternoon, any chance you'll be painting a little later on, my brain pan's a bit on the sensitive side.

"I could start when you show up," he replied with a sympathetic grin. "What with the acid, red lead and Gloucester white, chippin's the easy part of this job."

"For you," she snorted. "I did my chippin' last night. My head needs some peace and quiet today." She dumped her empty cup and crumpled paper towel under the sideboard in the plastic five-gallon oil bucket that served as a trash can. Her old Levis were almost worn through at the knees.

"O.K. Lenny Hill," she said with a hint of acceptance. "We'll be see'n ya then." She started up the ladder.

"About that beer?"

"Later boy, later," she replied, her battered topsiders following her into the sunlight.

"A female fisher named Franny," he thought, this could be awfully good or awfully bad. He didn't know squat about fishing. But the Coast Guard had provided him with a master's degree in metal maintenance. He followed her up the ladder. "Stick to what you know best," he concluded as he watched Miller's step-side Chevy pickup thread its way down the dock crowded with fishing gear and other vehicles.

No shortage of work here he thought, surveying his morning's achievement. The seventy-foot *Tecumseh* was a solid but old steel eastern-rigged longliner. Her carefree days were long since over. "If rust were gold," Lenny mused. Of course as long as the owner insisted on painting the old girl white, you couldn't expect to hide much rust. And once one's talked himself into a job he knows nothing about, it could be dangerous to quit because the man's boat was white and rusty. How about white and rusty after four years in the squeaky clean Coast Guard? Surely you understand, Cap. Surely you jest, Lenny.

Tom Martin, arms loaded, weaved his way down the gear-strewn dock, never taking his eyes off his pride and joy. The new man was still there, and making a respectable racket. He struggled to remember Hill's first name.

"Hello, Lenny," he called after a moment waiting for a pause in the clamorous chipping.

"Good morning, Captain," Lenny cheerily responded. "Would you like me to help you drop those things over the side?"

"Hate to see a good man miss a stroke." Tom paused, squatting to drop five white boxes marked "Mustad" from under his left arm to the dock. "The hooks will survive a bath, the laundry and radio might not."

Lenny reached toward Martin, grabbing the items that were handed to him in order of importance, depositing each on the fish hold hatch cover behind him.

"We really ought to put bait on these hooks before they go in the water," Lenny observed. Martin ignored his wit.

"Damn, son, you've done one helluva job here," the captain said once he'd gotten on deck and viewed Hill's handiwork. "Let me stash these goodies and I'll help you finish up so we won't miss happy hour."

"Happy hour is a mixed blessing when you're knockin' rust the next day," Hill observed ruefully.

"We're out of the woods tomorrow," the captain replied, "All you have to look forward to is taking ice."

"Some new pain threshold?"

"Only if you've been partying to excess," advised Martin. "Find yourself some sweet, young, innocent thing to take you home early," he proposed as he headed for the pilothouse with the hooks and VHF.

"Anything you say Br'er Fox," Lenny murmured.

When Tom returned, Lenny was busy saturating patches of rust-free metal with oily smelling red lead primer. Tom gave a gallon of semi-gloss Gloucester white a stir and started following Lenny's trail of red lead.

Half an hour later they paused to help Franny unload groceries. The food was already separated into milk crates of dairy, meat, vegetables, soft drinks and bakery products to go on ice in the fish hold and boxes of dry goods to go forward to the galley. When Lenny had handed the last box of dry goods below, Franny tossed him two frosty cans of beer.

"Cap'n looks a bit dehydrated," she warned.

Lenny rejoined Martin, who had resumed painting, and handed him a beer. Tommy smiled his thanks, took a swallow and continued painting. Lenny guzzled a long swallow until the cold liquid made his head ache. He put the can aside and gave his red lead a stir. In half an hour he was finished painting. Looking back at Martin's progress, he finished his beer.

"We'll have to cover the rest of this tomorrow when the lead's set up a little better," Tommy observed. "Why don't you stow the brushes and the paint. I'll lock up and we'll drag Fran over Malabar way for a cool one."

The front door of the Malabar Cafe was a massive oak hatch cover fitted with a 12-inch brassbound porthole. Red and green running lights flanked the entrance. Lenny struggled with the door. It seemed stuck like a boot in deep mud. Finally it opened, grudgingly. Lenny was glad to let Franny and Tom precede him into this dark, unfamiliar place. Inside light came from a hundred bottles of various colors in front of a mirror behind the bar. A portly, bald-headed bartender with a full black beard and eyebrows seemed to float from customer to customer with brimming mugs of brew and amber shots of liquor. Franny drifted off to a table filled with young candlelit faces with aviator's glasses perched on their foreheads. Tommy was taken aside by some whiskered individuals who might easily have modeled Greek captains' hats.

Lenny chose the anonymity of the bar. He took the last empty stool between two figures hunched over their drinks watching a small black and white television at the end of the bar. The huge man behind the bar floated over to him, stopped and stared with a mixture of curiosity and disdain. Lenny pointed to one of the frosty glasses next to him and put a dollar on the bar. The bartender brought him a mug and swept away his dollar bill.

He drank deeply. The taste of cold beer mingled with the sweet metallic remnants of rust that permeated his nasal passages making it all the sweeter. His eyes slowly became accustomed to the darkness of the bar. From behind the frothy rim of his mug he made out a dappled Narwhale poised on its tail at one end of the mirror behind the bar. "Love to chip rust with that sucker," he thought. The whale's head was lowered so that his spiraled tusk pointed horizontally along the top of the mirror, behind the top row of bottles. He was sighting along his tusk at an ebony mermaid perched at the other end of the mirror, eyes lowered demurely. Her body was anything but demure. Around her tail and traipsing across the bottom of the mirror was a procession of sea life in various lighter-than-air poses. "The bartender's children," thought Lenny. Crabs, lobsters, starfish, urchins, conch, eel and skate's egg cases, all shuffling along after their self-conscious leader. "Hors d'oeuvres," thought Lenny.

Lenny drank beer until he needed to pee. On his way back from the heavily perfumed urinal, he noticed the mural covering the entire wall opposite the bar. Depicted was a long thin strand of sand surrounded by wind-whipped seas. Closely spaced on both sides of the entire length of the spit were vessels of every description in various stages of disintegration. Broken tankers, tattered schooners, dismasted square-riggers, beached Novies and sanded-in draggers broadside to punishing storm seas. Along the length of the beach an historic procession of lifesaving equipment and personnel was deployed attempting the rescue of the stranded or resuscitation of forlorn survivors. Where the noble efforts of mercy had failed, commercial salvage and wrecking projects were in full swing and, sure enough, at the southern end of the spit, the legendary mooncusser, with lantern-toting nag to help keep the whole process primed. Beside each episode was etched the name of a vessel, the name of a captain, the month, the day and the year. In script at the lower right hand corner of the painting was written one word: MALABAR. Lenny could feel the hairs stand up on the back of his neck, and the familiar chill in the back of his legs. As he reclaimed his seat he couldn't help ponder the possibility that this bar could become his resting place when the sea was through chewing on him and spit him ashore.

The bartender kept putting beers in front of him pointing, in explanation, toward the candlelit tables. Hill drank beer until he couldn't pick himself out of the reflected collage of patrons and prancing sea life behind the bar. He pushed his last dollar across the bar, and slid off the barstool, carefully testing his legs as he eased awkwardly toward the door. It opened so easily he almost fell. He brushed past incoming patrons into the fresh cool darkness of the night.

The street back to the boat was deserted. A half moon made a twinkling path across the harbor between the channel islands. The smoke from a beach fire and snatches of song drifted fair wind to the mainland on a gentle southwester. Lenny had a sudden urge to leap from the sea wall and swim the moon's path to the island where he would emerge from the deep to warm himself in front of the beckoning bonfire to the shock and admiration of the merrymakers. Fortunately, the warmth and solitude of his bunk on *Tecumseh* got the best of him instead of the swift black currents beneath the path of the moon.

CHRISTINE & DAN

New Bedford

Six hours later Hill gripped the edge of his bunk. There was a humming noise in his spinning head. He was going to be sick for sure. A shaft of light momentarily bathed his face then moved on. He cautiously opened one eye. The sun was arching across the open hatch; they were underway!

He peered over the side of his bunk. The other bunks were empty. At the stove Franny was turning bacon in an iron skillet. Instantly, Lenny was starving. He climbed out of his bunk, waited for the port roll and made his way to the sink. He splashed water in his face, wiped it dry with a paper towel, and looked in the mirror on a cupboard door. When he looked at Franny again she was staring at the sizzling bacon, shaking her head.

"Coffee or O.J.?" she asked the cast iron skillet.

"O.J.," he croaked. She handed him an empty white china mug and pointed at the icebox.

"I've got Tommy's breakfast ready if you want to take the wheel."

Lenny poured himself a cup of orange juice and returned the carton to the icebox. Then, balancing his cup carefully, he headed up the forecastle ladder and made his way aft along the gently rolling deck. Propping the cup inside the pilothouse door, he smiled a greeting to Tommy, held up his index finger, and went aft to take a long leak.

Returning to the pilothouse, Lenny looked about to get his bearings. Tommy pointed to some tall mill stacks to starboard.

"New Bedford," and to some church steeples and a water tower further to starboard, "Fairhaven." For now you can head for that point with all the antenna towers. That's about three ten degrees. The tide's flooding so you want to pass to the right of any lobster gear. We're holding 170 degrees on the water temp and 32 pounds lube oil pressure at 1400 r.p.m." Tommy pointed at each instrument as he recited the readings. Lenny repeated each number as had been his habit in the service.

"I've got no one in sight," Tommy continued. "If you have a problem, idle her back," he said putting his hand on a chrome lever. "Take her out of gear if you hit anything and tap on the horn if you get to number four nun before I get back." Lenny nodded, "Three ten to number four."

"Keep an eye out behind you," Tommy warned as he picked up his coffee cup and tossed the spar-colored dregs into the cloudy green waters of the bay.

Martin was gone a good minute before *Tecumseh* fell off the light northerly breeze. Lenny nudged the wheel a half spoke to the right. *Tecumseh* stopped creeping, hesitated, then inched back toward 310 degrees. "Good girl," Lenny murmured as he eased off the half spoke in time for the bow to hang up on course.

Tommy was balancing a full cup of coffee as he stepped back into the pilothouse.

"Everything O.K?" he inquired inhaling the steam over the white mug.

"She's a real lady," Lenny reported. "Everything's as you left it, a quarter of a mile to number four."

"O.K.," Tommy replied. "Fran's got your breakfast." Lenny took his empty cup and growling stomach forward.

"How do you like your eggs?" Franny greeted him.

"Over easy," he replied, washing his hands and cup.

Two eggs sizzled in a small skillet as Franny looped the empty shells into the five-gallon bucket. Thirty seconds later she shook the pan to check their progress. Satisfied, she flipped the eggs, waited 15 seconds and folded them gently onto a hot plate already crowded with bacon, English muffins and home fries. Lenny smiled as he accepted his first square meal in a week.

"Coffee?" Franny asked. "Thank you," he replied handing her his cup.

The harbor unfolded before them as they breezed through the hurricane dike. The sun-drenched brick buildings of New Bedford, to the west, were in stark contrast to the cool, dark, tree-lined streets of Fairhaven to the east. New Bedford's skyline was punctuated with smokestacks and radio towers, Fairhaven's with church steeples and a sky-blue water tower. The contrast continued on the waterfront where conservative green and black hulls with stately white pilot houses aft, lined the docks to the east while vessels to the west, with pilot houses forward, were painted every conceivable color, no two alike.

Lenny stood by the pilothouse door. Franny and Tom scanned each side of the harbor with binoculars.

"Must be slow offshore," observed the skipper. "Louie, Butch and Artie, all in at the same time." As the end of the New Bedford side of the harbor came in sight, Tommy saw that the ice and fuel docks were jammed.

"Let's put two lines straight across to the last one in line there. Couple of fenders ought to do it." He put away his 7 by 50s.

Tecumseh slid alongside a pea green dragger with red rub rails and yellow pipe rigging. A group of four men in somber street clothes watched from on deck as Franny lassoed a cleat on the raised foredeck. Lenny searched in vain for a cleat aft and finally looked to Tommy for help.

"Put it through a scupper over the rail and back to the cleat," Tommy advised. Lenny dropped the eye of the mooring line over the rail until he could see the end through the scupper. Reaching through he grabbed the end and hauled back enough to reach his cleat as Tommy backed down on Franny's bow line to hold *Tecumseh* alongside the dragger. Once fast, Lenny quietly asked Fran.

"Who are these guys anyway?"

"Third world," she replied. "and very sensitive."

"Look like they've just come from a funeral, act like it too."

Having finally gotten fuel, Tommy had moved *Tecumseh* up behind another long liner at the ice dock when the pea green dragger moved silently alongside.

"Get some fenders in there quick!" Tommy yelled. Franny and Lenny scurried about with fenders as Tommy took a line from a man on the stern of the dragger that was, by now, between *Tecumseh* and the boat ahead of her. Tommy looked up to the bridge of the dragger; no one was in sight. He finally dropped the eye of the dragger's stern line over a cleat in the waist of *Tecumseh*. The silent fisherman aboard the dragger made his end of the already taut line fast, which finally stopped the forward progress of the vessel just as Tommy's harpoon stand kissed the dock.

"We'd like to use that stand to harpoon fish from," Tommy said to pea green's deck hand. The deck hand shrugged, lifting his palms skyward. Tommy turned away.

"Let's get her iced up before we get sunk," he said to his own crew as he started to undog the fish hold hatch.

Franny went below in her foul weather gear and handed up half the pen boards, two ice shavers and a shovel. Lenny helped Tom lower an eight-inch reinforced green plastic hose into the hatch until Franny motioned them to tie it off.

"How many?" called a coverall-clad figure from the second-floor window of the ice plant. Tommy held up both hands extending the fingers four times.

"Forty ton," the iceman acknowledged and disappeared. A sound like an air raid siren came from the hose, becoming muffled as it reached a crescendo. After a gallon of water spewed out, the rattle of chopped ice crackled through the system of pipes and hoses. The first wad of wet ice belched from the end of the hose as Franny leaned against the recoil to avoid being knocked across the "slaughterhouse." The wet ice came in fitful gobs that kept the hose bucking and Franny struggling to stay upright as she directed the slush about the bottom of each pen. After several minutes the ice came hard, dry and evenly, sending up a cloud of crystals and fog. Franny had the pens forward of the hatch filled when Tommy sent Lenny for his foul weather gear. The medicinal smell of the new Black Diamond gear gave him his first feeling of security. Tommy handed him a pair of dry gloves as Len lowered himself down the fish hold ladder.

The fish hold resounded with the whine of the ice blower and the chatter of ice bouncing off the plywood walls. Lenny tapped Franny on the shoulder. She turned as if frozen from the waist down. Lenny gulped in momentary horror at the hooded face of a 90-year-old woman peering out at him. Franny grinned at his shocked expression and shook her head to knock some of the frost off her hair and eyebrows. She pointed up at the hatch then forward toward some pens from which ice was spilling. Tommy was handing him pen boards to close the pens full of ice.

Franny motioned for Lenny to take the hose. Pointing to an empty pen, she grabbed the hood of his jacket and bellowed in his ear. "Don't bury the end of the hose." He nodded. His numbed ear felt warm for a moment, then wet and cold. A TV beer commercial went through his head. He worked the hose aft while Franny boarded up the full pens of ice and held a shovel under the stream of ice, diverting it around corners to places he couldn't reach with the hose. As he topped off the next to last pen, the whine of the ice blower became loud and clear, then slowly trailed off in pitch and intensity until it died with a guttural snarl.

"Whew," blurted Lenny, "that's a blast. What's with the empty pen?"

"Bait." Franny caught the ice shaver and extra shovel Tommy dropped to her.

"You guys need anything up the street?" he asked. Franny looked to Lenny who shook his head.

"Nada," she replied.

"Well let's see if we can get out of here," he said, handing down the ice-hold ladder.

Lenny and Franny took their lines off the dock and Tommy came slow ahead with the helm hard to port. Slowly the dragger outside them eased into the channel. Slowly the gap between *Tecumseh* and the boats astern widened.

"Drop that stern line when she goes slack," he told Franny, taking one last look behind him. Tommy took the engine out of gear and waited for Franny to flip the dragger's mooring line off the cleat as he reversed the wheel. Free at last, he gave the engine a short powerful kick astern so that *Tecumseh* followed the rudder to starboard when he took her out of gear.

After a short stop at the water barge, they headed for the breakwater. Franny took the wheel while Tommy and Lenny painted over red lead with Gloucester white. As they arrived back at the dock a white refrigerated truck slowly backed down the now deserted pier. A slender, dungaree clad figure with meticulously manicured Fu Manchu slid out of the cab.

"You guys want this bait today?"

"Might's well," replied Tommy, exchanging quizzical looks with Franny. The driver opened the back of the truck revealing a rounded pile of corrugated cardboard boxes. Many were broken open. Four half-frozen mackerel fell on deck.

"What the fuck is this?" demanded Martin.

"Load must have shifted," the driver offered.

“Shift my ass!” Tommy snorted, “that bait was loaded just the way it’s laying.”

“Well, it didn’t happen on my watch,” the driver whined. “Do you want it or not?”

“Yah, we want it,” Tommy conceded, “but if you try to drop another load like this on us we’ll bait up in New Bedford and watch you try to return your mess to the freezer.” He turned to Franny, “Pack the good stuff in the pen, leave the broken boxes in the slaughterhouse to use the first couple of nights.” She nodded.

Departure

Having packed and iced the bait, Lenny and Franny emerged from the fish hold as a dark green Mustang convertible pulled up next to the boat. The tattered rag-top did little to mute the electronic complaint blasting from within. "I can't get no, satisfaction." declared the vocalist, no matter how he "tried and tried."

Fanny checked her watch. "Right on time."

A large black dog of Labrador persuasion exploded through the shards of plexiglass that had once been the rear window of the convertible. He hit the dock running and lunged along the cap-rail, flushing a dozen resting herring gulls from their piling perches, one at a time. The dog emitted guttural growls and snorts as each bird made its escape with as little effort as possible. Reaching the end of the dock, he threw himself with wild abandon, in pursuit of the last bird. Following the path of its predecessors, the bird glided to the harbor's surface, caught the light southwester, and wheeled in a tight circle, returning to the piling from which it had been flushed.

"Go get'm Coke!" Tommy encouraged the briskly swimming canine.

Two people got out of the car. The driver, tall and dark, wearing expensive Polaroids, a white undershirt, black jeans and rubber shower sandals, took the keys from the ignition to open the trunk. He took out a pair of knee boots and a small laundry bag, which he dropped on deck. Slamming the trunk shut, he embraced a short, solid, honey blond in a black, thigh-length T-shirt covered with bigger than life, liver-colored lips. Her hands, with gold fingernails, met at the small of the tall man's back. They slowly migrated down the back of his beltless jeans where they became tightly secured in the unused belt loops.

"Jesus!" exclaimed the man, twisting free from her grasp. He tossed her the car keys.

"Fuck off Angie," he said. Angie stifled a giggle.

"You want these lines?" he asked turning to Tommy.

"All but the after spring, Sam," Tommy answered.

Angie, in an exaggerated pout, glued herself to a piling next to the pilothouse while Sammy dropped the lines except for the spring and climbed onto the whaleback as Tommy put *Tecumseh* slow ahead to push the stern away from the dock.

"Wake me when it's over," said Sammy as he passed Franny on his way down the foc'sle doghouse. Tommy took the engine out of gear and the spring line went slack.

"Angie, you're going to get seagull shit on your ninnies." Franny warned. Angie backed away from her piling as Franny jerked the spring line, flipping the eye of the mooring line off Angie's piling into the water. Lenny eyed the front of Angie's T. shirt checking for seagull shit or melted tar from the piling. Franny interrupted further research by knocking his wind out with a well aimed, tightly coiled mooring line.

"Under the lifeboat," she whispered. He took one last look at Angie. She returned his gaze, examining him with the confidence of a cat contemplating a cornered rodent. He woke up desperately reaching for the mooring line Franny was already carrying aft. She recoiled, then gave him the line rolling her eyes heavenward.

"Don't hurt yourself," she warned. He staggered aft with the two heavy lines carefully watching his feet to avoid tripping. Franny was waiting at the top of the ladder to the turtleback where the lifeboat was lashed in its cradle. He handed the lines up to her. She took them one at a time then turned with them, shaking her head, toward the lifeboat. Tommy backed *Tecumseh* away from the dock and turned her for the outer harbor. Lenny glanced back toward the dock. Just before entering the street, the departing convertible paused long enough for a very wet dog to leap onto the trunk and disappear through the missing rear window.

Rounding the harbor entrance buoy, Tommy headed down the sound, turned on the autopilot and started stowing loose tools and paperwork that had accumulated during the layover. Franny showed up half an hour later.

"You got a rare burger on the back of the stove, we headed for the hooter?"

"Yah," Tommy answered, "keep Gay Head a couple of points to port, look out for the traffic coming out of Quick's. You may need some lights before I get back."

The green flasher of Devil's Bridge bell buoy reflected on a ripple left by the diminishing southwester as *Tecumseh* surged fair tide past the buoy, munching into swells built up by the ebbing current. The sunset's afterglow silhouetted the Elizabeth Islands to the west as Tommy put his coffee mug in the cup holder next to the wheel.

"Think the dune hopper is ready to stand a watch?" Tommy asked Franny.

"Ready as he'll ever be," she replied. "I think Len got liberated before the idea of one man, one job had a chance to sink in," she chuckled. They were both silent for a moment thinking of the first watch each had stood: a course to steer, three radios to listen to, half a dozen instruments to watch, a lookout to keep and the lives of four people to protect.

"Well, call him when you get past Nomans," he said, interrupting her thoughts.

"Let him look for 68-degree water and follow it 'til he calls me at twelve. If tomorrow's a good day, we might as well be looking for a few finners."

"Sounds like R & R," Franny agreed. "Sammy will appreciate that too."

First Watch

It was ten o'clock when she called Lenny. He splashed some water in his face, poured hot coffee into a cup with a couple of spoons of powdered chocolate and headed for the pilothouse. Franny reeled off the course, gauge readings and Tommy's instructions for Lenny's watch. She pointed out the surface temperature gauge prominently positioned over the compass.

"You want to steer 140 degrees until the temperature drops to 68, then hold it by steering right 20 degrees for every degree of temperature you're under 68, and left 20 degrees for every degree of temperature you're over 68. You follow that?"

"Sounds almost logical," Lenny answered playing dumb. "Cold water's on the bank to our left, warm's offshore to our right."

"Very good!" Franny gushed with a wrinkled brow. "One detail; don't go west of 180 or north of 090."

"Got it," said Lenny. "One twenty to 68 degrees sea surface, then hold it. Who do I call at midnight?"

"Call Tommy, he wants to listen to the weather to make sure we've got looking weather for tomorrow. Did anyone tell you about the engine and bilge alarms?"

Lenny shook his head.

"They're hooked up to the same bell." She pointed to the crimson electrical appliance jammed between all the others on the after wall of the pilothouse.

"If that sucker rings, you'll probably have a heart attack. After that, throw off the toggle switch to the engine room. If the bell keeps ringing you have high water, if it stops, you have a hot engine or low oil pressure, shame on you for not watching your instruments close enough. In any case, idle the engine and let the skipper deal with it. You got all that?"

"I think so, just got to remember there aren't five guys standing around to catch it if I screw up."

"Exactly. Call Tommy if any boats get close enough to make out their running lights or if it fogs up." She paused, then added, "Call me if you have any questions."

"Gotcha," Lenny said. And finally, "Who's Sammy anyway?"

"He's our railman harpooner," Fanny answered.

"Was he having a slack attack today or is he always that way?" Lenny ventured.

"Sammy Santos doesn't give a shit for convention," declared Franny, with unvarnished admiration. "You'll see what a valuable attribute that can be before this trip is over."

"Gotcha," Lenny said again. "And thanks."

Franny nodded, picked up her coffee mug and headed forward, checking the navigation lights before disappearing down the forecastle doghouse.

Lenny adjusted the binnacle light as low as it would go while still enabling him to read the compass card. He peered into the darkness, acutely aware of how much less he could see from this pilothouse than he could from the bow or flying bridge of a cutter. He took a long swallow of his chocolate coffee, then checked the squelch adjustments on the two very high frequency (VHF) radios and adjusted the volume of each so it could be heard over the noise of the engine coming through the floor of the pilothouse. One set monitored the international calling and distress channel 16. The other scanned 35 safety and communications channels. Both were silent except for a brief announcement from Camden Marine Operator saying she was packing it in 'til seven in the morning and "wishing all stations good fishing and a pleasant evening." Lenny smiled, he wondered if the operator dropped by Cappy's for a cool one after wishing all the boys on the wagon offshore a pleasant evening. He wanted to tell her to have one for him but decided he was too busy and headed in the wrong direction. His decision was confirmed moments later when a large light loomed close aboard on the port bow. Lenny's heart was in his mouth. The light was too close to avoid. He was about to throw the wheel hard to starboard when he recognized his lopsided friend from the night before.

"Jesus Moon!" he cursed out loud.

When his heart slowed down, Lenny marveled at the variety of new things he had done since he ignored the call of that same heavenly body 24 short hours earlier. Suddenly he remembered the sea water temperature gauge he was supposed to be watching. It read 67 and was dropping. He brought the wheel right a spoke to settle up on 140. "I'm going to have to give up daydreaming," he thought, watching the black needle hover just below 67.

Lenny set about analyzing his job. Simply put, he must keep the engine healthy so he could steer a course to follow the temperature and avoid hitting anything. Four steps, of which steering needed the most attention.

He finally settled on a routine which took his attention from steering to engine instruments, back to steering to lookout, back to steering and finally to temperature gauge. By the end of his two-hour watch the procedure was almost habit. If he got bored he decided he could put in a little "free time" segment to add variety and alleviate monotony but as yet he was anything but bored. In fact it was after twelve when he noticed the time. "Add a time check," he thought, and went aft to turn on the red light over the chart table. Tommy's eyes were open. Lenny waved his hand in front of Tommy as if checking the response of one comatose. Tommy blinked. Lenny held up one finger. Tommy's lips made a "one." Lenny held up two fingers. Tommy lips made a "two."

"Twelve o'clock and all's well," Lenny smiled. Tommy nodded.

Arriving in the pilothouse with his coffee, Tommy jabbed the scanner touch pad and caught the VHF National Weather Service broadcast in the middle of the coastal forecast out of Hyannis. "... early fog burning off by noon. Variable winds becoming onshore."

"Perfect day for looking, Lenny, what have you done for us in the temperature department?"

"Cranking away at it, Cap, that edge must look like some kind of centipede."

"Ya did good." Tommy saw that the temperature gauge read between 68 and 69.

"Why don't you take a snooze and I'll hang'er up next to the corner buoy so we'll be on top of the mother lode in the morning but out of the shipping lane 'til then."

"Sounds good to me. Your gauges are O.K, and I'll check the lights on my way forward. The visibility doesn't seem to be all that good. I haven't seen anything since the mother moon popped out from behind a fog bank or cloud and scared the livin' shit out of me."

"Yah." Tommy turned the radar power knob to standby. "We're getting close to the South Channel fog machine. It'll burn off by the time old swordfish has a belly full and decides to fin out to warm up, 'bout noon I figure, right about slack water . . . perfect." His voice trailed off. Lenny wanted to ask a dozen questions about what seemed so logical to Tommy, but Martin had turned on the autopilot and had his face buried in the rubber radar hood. Lenny's bunk called.

"We'll get you in the morning," he said as he collected his coffee cup. Lenny paused beside the forecastle doghouse. The navigation lights had haloes around them, it was getting foggy for sure. He gave Tommy a thumbs up and went below.

A counter light dimly illuminated the galley. Franny's glistening cast-iron Shipmate stove radiated dry warmth, a welcome contrast to conditions on deck. Lenny washed out his cup. The engine was only background noise here. The comforting distant hum playing second fiddle to the slap and swish of the bow wave pushed aside by *Tecumseh*'s straight stem. There was always motion, but it soon became a comfort, especially once in your bunk. Lenny kicked off his shoes and crawled under a light blanket. He loved his bunk. On the cutter a steel pipe frame had held his mattress. It was too shallow and provided only a cold railing to hang on to when seas threatened to throw you out. The sides of the built-in wooden forecastle bunks of *Tecumseh* were a foot high and provided an instant sense of security. Lenny's surroundings reminded him of a hunting camp, which in fact it was. He was wrestling with Franny's description of Sammy and how "not giving a shit" could contribute to the success of a trip when he drifted off to sleep.

In the pilot house, Tommy picked up two radar targets at eight miles that were obscured by fog. One of them had to be the Davis South Shoal buoy. He headed to the north of the nearest target to be sure to be inside the turning buoy, safe from Boston-bound traffic. The water temperature dropped and the fog thickened as *Tecumseh* neared the radar targets. At a range of three miles Tommy slowed the engine to idle and took it out of gear. Going below, he pumped the fish hold free of ice water. Returning to the pilothouse he watched the radar long enough to see that the green blips south of him were not changing their range or bearing. Satisfied, he shut down the engine and radar. His legs tingled with the absence of vibration from the engine below. He snapped off the engine-room lights and port and starboard running lights. This left *Tecumseh*'s two white range lights and stern light making misty arcs that gently fanned the fog swirling through the rigging as lazy swells gently rolled under her hull. Tommy turned the scanner volume down and the channel 16 radio up. Outside the chartroom porthole he could hear the cheeping of Wilson's petrels attracted to the stern light. He set the alarm on a beat-up Westclock for five thirty and crawled into his bunk fully clothed.

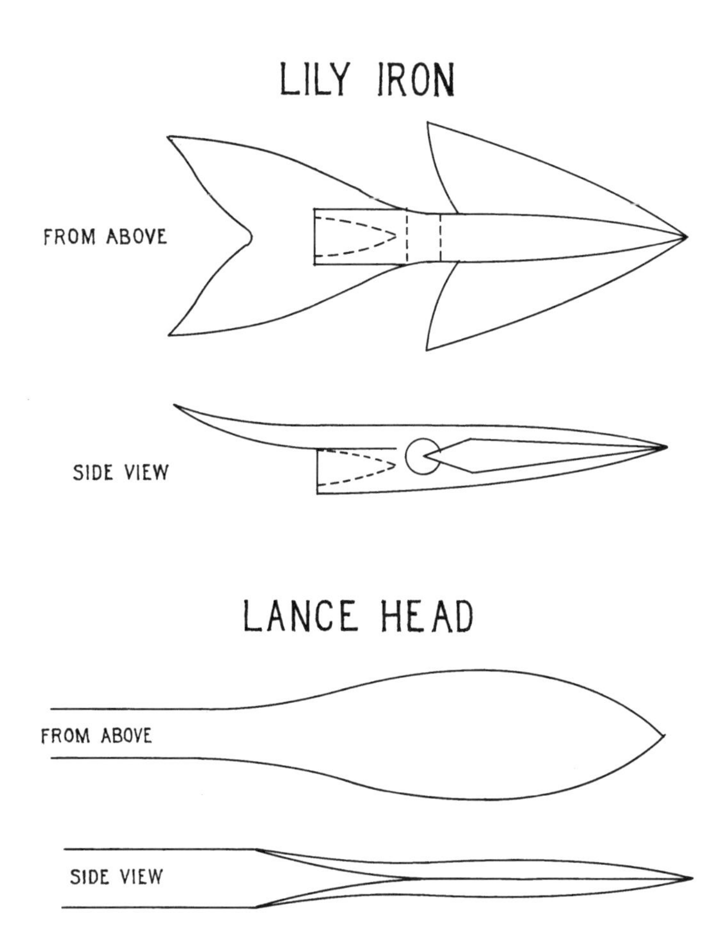

Day of the Harpoon

In what seemed like an instant later, the Westclock rang him awake. A suggestion of light came through the porthole across the chartroom. He rolled out of his bunk, wincing as the bones in his feet protested the second early call in two days. Staggering to the pilothouse, he peered into the swirling fog that was collecting on the rigging aloft and creating a steady drizzle on deck. "Couple of hours to clearing," he thought as he turned off the range lights. Increasing the volume on the scanner, he hobbled back to the chartroom where his stocking feet followed him back into his warm bunk.

The smell of fried sausage heralded Franny's arrival in the chartroom two hours later.

"Breakfast's just about ready," she announced, "Gonna be a beautiful day."

"Thanks," he replied, "Coming."

Tommy looked from his clock to the porthole. The fog had turned peach color. "Time to get moving," he murmured as he slid into his boat shoes. Passing through the pilothouse he turned the radar to STANDBY, then shuffled forward to the forecastle.

Franny was topping off his plate with a couple of sunny side eggs as he came down the ladder. He took the hot plate from her and joined Lenny at the table. Len had finished his eggs, sausage and home fries and was capping an English muffin with copious amounts of orange marmalade.

Tommy poked an egg yoke with a muffin of his own, and looked at Len. "So did you manage to get any sleep?"

"Must have tossed and turned for all of half a minute. Thought I'd never get any rest. Hadn't been to sleep for more than half an hour before Fran started makin' these awful smells. Like to ruin a man's appetite as well as what rest he can snatch between watches," Lenny devoured half a muffin in one bite. Franny never took her eyes off a skillet of scrambled eggs.

"Now Sammy there," Lenny motioned with the other half of his muffin toward the lump in a lower bunk that hadn't moved for 12 hours, "there's a light sleeper. Don't you think it's time to look for a pulse?"

"Only thing that'll get Sam up and at 'em will be a swordfish. When he moves, start looking for finners." Tommy studied the back of Sam's head over the rim of his coffee cup.

Franny joined them at the table with a plate of scrambled eggs and toast. She took a long drag on a mug of orange juice. "Foggy weather's best spent resting Sammy's eyes. When ol' purple goes deep you want Sammy up there with a clear head and an empty stomach."

"Yah," Tommy added. "Hungry Sam and well fed ol' purple, what a beautiful sight."

"But I thought swordfish were gray," Lenny said.

"Oh, he is by the time he gets to the office." Franny explained. "Complete with a pin stripe of a lateral line when he's dead. But when he's alive he can be any color that suits his surroundings, from black to blue to bronze to silver or purple, most usually a combination of the above."

Lenny shook his head. "This I gotta see."

"Me too," said Tommy as he took his dishes to the sink. "I'm going to jog her south and rig the stand, you guys ought to be ready to do some lookin' shortly. We've got someone laid to near the South Shoal buoy, might a' been on fish yesterday. Look out for a plane."

In the pilothouse Tommy studied the radar. There were still two targets south of *Tecumseh* but the distance between them was widening. "Someone's on the move," he said to himself, heading for the engine room.

The light green diesel had cooled off. Tommy checked the water level in the heat exchanger and pulled the engine oil dipstick. It read LOW. Tommy drew a quart of 30 weight from a yellow tank and watched the amber fluid stream slowly from the oil can spout into the engine.

"Easy day," he advised the engine. "Just run smooth and quiet."

"Let's go get 'em," he added after checking the clutch oil dipstick.

Back in the pilothouse Tommy could see some light blue sky coming through the silver haze overhead. He pushed the starter button and was answered by the familiar staccato of a cool diesel. Checking the overboard discharge from the engine, he made his way forward to rig the harpoon stand. Everything forward was cold, wet and slippery. A dark, bat-like creature fluttered out of his way, hobbling as if crippled, along the scupper ahead of him. Tommy cupped his hands and captured the soft, struggling creature. The petrel grabbed his thumb with its hooked beak with the strength of a fiddler crab.

"Easy, big feller, you're going to need that strength," he murmured as he checked the breeze. Walking to the port rail, he launched the bird with an upward thrust of his hands.

"Go find me a swordfish slick," he instructed the ball of frantically flapping feathers that suddenly regained its composure just before hitting the water. Zigzagging to evade predators or to get its bearings, the bird decided where to go and was lost from sight in the fog.

Tommy untied the keg and tag lines that led to the ends of the harpoon. He then carefully crabbed out the 20-foot harpoon bowsprit and untied the business end of the harpoon. He checked to see that the bronze dart was not jammed on the iron rod that tipped the end of the 16-foot aluminum pole. Following the keg line to the other end of the harpoon he pulled the slack in a bight through a stiff plastic becket that kept the dart from falling off the iron rod until it was in a fish. Finally he rotated the pole so that the keg line, which would lead from the dart to the float, was not wrapped around the tag line which would retrieve the harpoon. That done, he retied the harpoon with two slip knots on each side of the pulpit waist band. Back aboard, he made sure there was enough slack in the keg line to keep the harpoon from fetching up before reaching a deep fish. Satisfied, he jammed a bight of keg line in a becket on the mast stay over a carefully coiled tub of line topped with a bright orange plastic float measuring 40 inches across.

Back in the pilothouse Tommy observed the engine temperature needle coming off the peg. He eased the clutch lever forward and watched the compass card start to move. Holding the wheel with one hand he turned the radar power knob from STANDBY to ON and watched the heading marker swing slowly toward the closest target south of him. Easing the helm, he checked *Tecumseh*'s turn as it approached the heading to the target and noted the compass course. Dialing up that course on the autopilot, he snapped on the power switch over his head. The wheel started turning in small jerky mechanical adjustments as Tommy checked the radar confirming the autopilot's accuracy. He leaned on the throttle lever and listened as the chortle below him smoothed into a purr.

Down forward Lenny finished washing Franny's ironware and put it on the stove to dry. She covered a dish of leftover potatoes and sausage that she put in the icebox.

"What's the uniform of the day?" Lenny asked.

"Oilskins, I guess," Franny answered. "No sense being cold and wet" She handed him a pair of drugstore Polaroids and two of the four chocolate bars she snaked from a hiding place deep in the back of a cupboard under the sideboard.

"Might be awhile before your next meal," she advised.

Lenny watched Franny slip into a heavy wool green-and-black checkered shirt. He rummaged in his drawer to find his service turtleneck as she went up the ladder. The heat from the galley had warmed their foul weather gear hanging in the doghouse. Feeling overdressed Lenny struggled to keep his footing as he followed Franny. She had already climbed the rigging and squirmed into a mast hoop. A seat hung from the hoop with a cross stay beneath to rest her boots. As Lenny climbed, engine exhaust became louder, masking the sound of the approaching aircraft. Lenny struggled to get his shoulders, bulky with foul weather gear, through the mast hoop opposite Franny. He took one last look aft before turning to sit down and looked straight into the prop of an onrushing airplane. For a brief second he couldn't believe his eyes, then he saw the look of panic on the pilot's face as he threw up a forearm to protect himself from the inevitable collision. Lenny grabbed Franny's arm, ducked down, and moaned, "Hang on."

"WHARRRRROOOOOOOM." The roar was punctuated by prop blast that shook the mast, then almost total silence as the pilot throttled back and banked around for another approach.

"*Hawkeye*, you asshole," hissed Franny as she pulled Lenny around so that he faced forward and could sit down.

"He did that on purpose?" Lenny asked in disbelief.

"Yeah," Franny exhaled with exasperation.

"Waits until you get all suited up and settled comfortable then tries to sneak up and scare you so you'll have to take a pee. Don't pay any attention to him, he knows you're new aboard."

Tommy leaned out of the pilothouse. "I told you to look out for a plane," he chided, unable to conceal his amusement. He tuned the VHF to channel 70 and picked up the mike.

"*Hawkeye*, *Hawkeye*, *Tecumseh*; and what brings you out to these parts so early my man, a little donut run?"

"Donuts? Hell, I need some of Fran's biscuits to sop up this pea soup. You seen my boat?"

"There's someone down next to the turning buoy," Tommy offered. "Where'd you leave them last night?"

"Twenty-eight fathoms, Tommy, guess they came inside to get clear of the big boys when it fogged up." *Hawkeye* once more closed on *Tecumseh*'s port yardarm.

"Try four miles south by east of us," Tommy suggested, "and let me know if you see any clear spots on the way."

"That's 'what the world needs now,'" *Hawkeye* sang as he glided quietly past the mainmast.

His stealth was rewarded with an Italian salute from the smaller figure at *Tecumseh*'s masthead.

"Your cook's got an attitude problem," *Hawkeye* advised Tommy, "but I think I found a couple of guys walkin' on the fog down here. Doesn't look like I'll be doing them much good for a bit."

"*Phalarope*, *Phalarope*. *Hawkeye*. Ya pickin' me up Cap'n Ed?"

"Marnin' *Hawk*," a sleepy voice replied. "Didn't expect you so early. No visibility around here. Why don't you go find that warm water from yesterday? Should clear there as quick as anywhere."

Fran and Lenny had watched *Hawkeye* disappear ahead of them then reappear in the distance as he banked around another masthead sticking up through the fog.

"These people must have had some kind of day yesterday to be wired this early with this kind of visibility," Franny speculated.

Hawkeye circled the men in the rigging south of *Tecumseh* one more time before heading south ahead of them.

During a two hour run south the fog began to burn off. Shearwaters, which had been cutting in and out of Tommy's circle of visibility, were finally in sight everywhere, searching for schools of

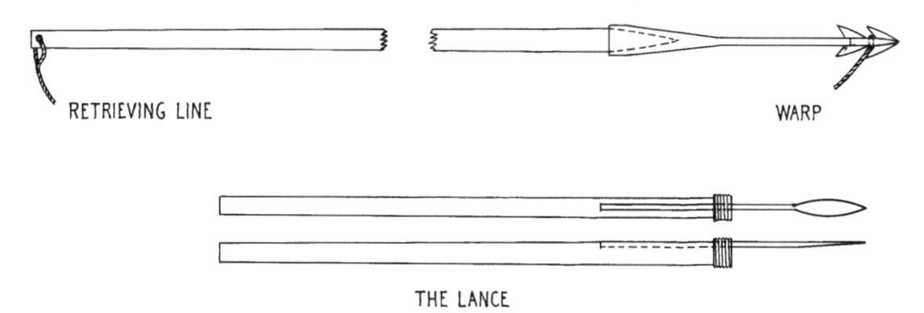

small fish forced to the surface by larger fish feeding on them from below. He took his window squeegee outside and wiped the fog droplets from the windows. Back inside, he opened both pilothouse doors and took a piece of lens tissue from the chart table to clean his 7 by 50s.

Sammy Goes to Work

A white coffee cup appeared at the top of the forecastle ladder followed by Sammy's head of curly black hair. His face reflected the brightness of the morning. He put the cup on deck and disappeared. Moments later he reemerged wearing a red and black checkered wool shirt and equipped with amber Polaroids. A greasy brown cap with a long, shiny, black visor was secured to his head with a chin strap. Sipping his coffee, he slowly made his way to the fish-hold hatch cover, all the while reading the ocean to his left and right as if it were that morning's issue of the *Wall Street Journal.* Leaving his cup on the hatch, he disappeared aft without acknowledging Tommy's existence. Reappearing, he took another swallow of coffee, put down the cup and reached up, putting both hands over the boom. Slowly, he lifted his feet off the deck and hung there.

Tommy was scanning the horizon when he heard Sammy's feet hit the deck. He looked down to see one of Sammy's arms at his side, the other extended toward the starboard bow as if offering to shake some imaginary hand. Tommy peered to starboard, pulling the wheel several spokes to the right. Sammy moved to the rail, slowly bringing his arm to the left until he was pointing straight ahead. Tommy held *Tecumseh* on the course while Sammy sprang from the whaleback to the harpoon stand. He untied the harpoon with two sharp tugs at the restraining lanyards. Swinging the harpoon, he pointed it slightly to starboard. Tommy adjusted his course to the new heading.

Several minutes passed before Tommy made out two sickle-shaped objects riding low in the water, one in front of the other. They were black, about the size of shearwater wings. The fish below them was heading left so Tommy eased the wheel left to get out ahead of it. Sammy wagged the harpoon up and down to indicate he agreed with the adjustment. The seconds dragged by as Tommy struggled with minute wheel adjustments that would put Sammy over the fish without any last second maneuver that might rattle either the fish or harpooner. Finally the fish was lost from Tommy's view from the pilothouse and simultaneously emerged from the surface glare for the observers at the masthead. For only a brief moment could they observe the huge electric purple body with neon blue trim. Their trance was interrupted by Sammy's stretching torso reaching with right arm erect on the butt of the harpoon; willing himself to a position directly over the quarry before it spooked. The moment came and down drove Sammy's right arm. The fish disappeared. Tommy spun the wheel hard left and threw the engine in reverse. Sammy pulled the tag line to retrieve the harpoon. Franny, down from aloft, held the float over the side with her right hand and checked the drag on the line pile in the tub with her left.

"I think you hurt him, Sam."

He laid the harpoon on the whaleback and joined her, taking the line.

"She's backboned, Cap," he told Martin. "We can give it a try when you get her around." Tommy took the engine out of reverse and kicked her ahead to get the harpoon line out from under the bow. Sammy gently checked the progress of line overboard. Slowly the line came clear of the hull and Sammy led it through the rail-roller and started to pull. There was no struggle at the other end of the line, just a tantalizingly heavy weight. Sammy pulled patiently hand over hand. The fish was his. Franny hung up the float and coiled the harpoon line back into the tub as Sammy hauled.

Five minutes passed before the line started to tend away from the boat at an ever-increasing angle. Suddenly a long black sword broke the surface followed by the huge eyes and head of a large swordfish. Slowly the fish's head and bill fell back into the water as its body and extended pectoral broke the surface.

"Three hundred, three twenty five," wheezed Sammy as the fish started to plane toward the stern of the boat. Tommy put the engine in reverse blowing the fish forward with the wheel wash. Franny was ready with a gaff as the fish came to the gate in the rail. She struck hard, hooking and lifting the four-foot tail from the water high enough for Tommy to encircle it with a loop of the landing hoist line. Tommy gave the loop to Sammy to hold while he engaged the cathead and took three turns on the shiny bronze spool. Lenny's perch shook as Tommy took a strain on the hoist that was led through a block clamped to the triadic stay over the fish hold hatch.

Slowly the great shape emerged from its element. Twin lobes of the graceful tail were even with the top of the pilothouse when the bill finally cleared the rail. Gently, Tommy lowered the prize while Sammy held the bill and Franny dampened the swing of the fish responding to a slight swell. No sooner had the fish come to rest on deck than Sammy had cut off the bill with a meat saw. Franny removed the tail strap and cut off the tail with a blunt nosed slime knife. Together, they rolled the fish over as Fran deftly cut off pectoral, anal and dorsal fins. They slid the body up along the port rail and covered it with burlap bags soaked with the deck hose.

"Let's go find another," Tommy sang out as he headed for the pilothouse.

Franny shed her foul weather gear and rejoined Lenny aloft. Together they watched Sammy re-rig the harpoon and snap a small bos'n chair on to the frame of the pulpit in which he took a seat.

"And that's it?" Lenny blurted. "That's the ultimate rush of swordfish harpooning?"

"You don't get a rush in this business until you fuck up," Franny shot back. "If Sammy backboned every fish, it would be a bloody bore; but as it is he only numbs every third fish so there's still plenty of opportunity for working and jerking and hauling back empty irons. Now there's a rush you can look forward to."

Lenny told himself to shut up and learn something about this seemingly primitive method of fishing.

"Which reminds me," Franny continued, "we should be looking for underwater fish from up here now that Sammy has joined the skipper looking for finners. Our non-glare radius is ten times what theirs is."

"Cool," said Lenny as he struggled out of his foul weather gear. It was getting warm at the masthead as the sea flattened under the midday sun. Long slicks developed stretching from southeast to northwest. Shearwaters gathered in flocks to wash and preen and search patches of weed for hidden edibles. Petrels gathered in similar flocks moving only when threatened by *Tecumseh*'s bow wave.

The second fish was a long time coming. As they searched the depths, Franny pointed out swordfish veils, light purple-gray gelatinous masses that floated near the surface. "They're supposed to mean that there are swordfish around, but really they're goosefish eggs. Don't ask me where that one got started." They saw ocean sunfish, with identical dorsal and anal fins, sculling away from the bow wave. "Now they're supposed to eat jelly fish," Franny said, "but I'll bet they eat swordfish veils too." And finally they started seeing "bluedog" sharks, one after another, meandering aimlessly. "The tail's the secret," Franny instructed. "It flops from side to side and will reflect the sun. Never so with the swordfish or marlin."

Lenny gazed into the water. "I feel like I'm part of some kind of costume ball," he reflected. "The fish comes equipped with a formidable snout so the fisherman apes him with the long-billed cap and puts a bowsprit on his boat. Now are these things necessities of the business or are we trying to make the fish believe we're one of them?"

Franny dug inside the front of her shirt. "Methinks it's time for your candy bar." A distant slap interrupted their snack. They looked up to see a geyser of white water returning to the ocean's surface a mile away.

"Breacher!" howled Sammy looking back toward the pilothouse to make sure Tommy was awake. Tommy brought *Tecumseh* to the new heading. They steamed for half a mile, Sammy poised, harpoon in hand, Lenny and Fran straining to catch a glimpse of the jumper. Tommy's tense voice came over the P.A. system. "I can't see him. Did anyone see a sword or was it a sunfish?" Sammy didn't turn to answer; he just shook the harpoon.

Tommy eased back on the throttle, not wanting to run the fish down. They idled along for another minute before he took the engine out of gear. *Tecumseh* drifted, nothing moved. Tommy was about give up the wait when, not 50 yards away, a fin clipped the surface making tight figure eights as if looking for something it had lost. Tommy had *Tecumseh* in gear, slowly accelerating the engine as he put on enough rudder to intercept the fish, which kept weaving around making it impossible to do anything but run right at her. By now both dorsal and tail fins were high in the water and the fish became more agitated with their approach. As Sammy came over the fish, it gave a kick with its tail sending a great fan of water flying. Sammy reacted instinctively, throwing the harpoon ahead of the fish. In that same instant it was gone. Coils of line stood two feet high over the keg line tub as the fish raced away. Tommy reached the tub on the run as it emptied. Throwing the polyball, he ducked in case it fetched up on something and parted off. The ball came out from under the bow and boiled off, leaving a rooster tail behind.

"Nice shot, Sammy!" Tommy handed the harpooner another dart and put the attached keg line in the empty tub on the hauling table.

"Think we can catch up with him?" Sammy was smiling.

"We did once," Tommy answered. "I'll talk to the engineer."

They got underway, steaming southeast, keeping the polyball in sight, hoping it would lead them to another fish. Tommy listened to *Hawkeye* put the *Phalarope* on their fourth fish. They were having a fair day but seeing only half the fish they saw the day before. Tommy could hear a hint of frustration in the radio communications. Six fish would have been a good day if they hadn't had a dozen the day before. They knew the body of fish had moved. Looking the wrong way tomorrow would mean a wasted day. The decision had to be made before the plane left.

Aloft, Franny watched the mainmast shadow lengthen. The polyball continued its relentless passage southeast. "This looks like a long haul. I'm going to drop below and start some supper so we can schedule a quick kink before midnight madness."

"I'll keep track of *Hawkeye* for you," Lenny promised, handing her the borrowed Polaroids. Franny handed them back.

"That asshole," she confirmed, sliding out of the mast hoop and starting down the shrouds. Below she adjusted the oil valve to the maximum and started increasing the blower volume on the Shipmate. She put two cups of rice in a saucepan of salt water and put it on the warmest corner of the stove.

Lenny gazed out at the horizon. They had left the *Phalarope* behind with the birds, sharks, slicks and weed. The ocean here was empty except for the orange polyball that rode a bit higher in the water but continued its offshore trek. A gentle southwester covered the sea surface with ripples that diminished underwater visibility from the masthead. Lenny searched for anything to break the monotony of the empty seascape; anything that might lend perspective so he might determine how far from his perch he might hope to see the fin of a swordfish.

At the end of each sweeping search his eyes settled on the or-

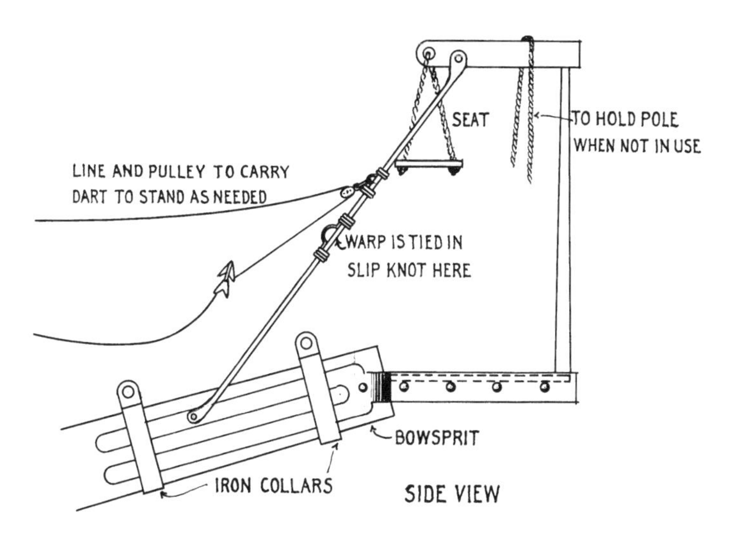

THE STAND OR PULPIT

ange float. He speculated about the possibility that carrots had been created orange to make them easier to find, subsequently resulting in better eyesight for the finder. It seemed quite obvious that the orange had been discovered before the carrot or the carrot would have been called orange. It didn't explain why lemons weren't called yellows. He wondered if anyone actually used a carrot tied to a stick to encourage some beast of burden toward a secondary goal. Surely it couldn't provoke more dogged persistence than that with which *Tecumseh* pursued this promised prize. Lenny wondered about the fish. Did she have landmarks by which she measured her progress? Was she enroute to the drop-off hoping to have enough strength left to sink the float when she reached deep enough water? Or was she hoping to find some lobster gear in which to foul the keg line and pull the dart? Lenny was mesmerized by the consistency of the buoy's progress, its shimmering bow wave and dark swirling wake. He put his ear to the mast to listen for a message from the fish. What he heard was the hum of the distant diesel idling along just fast enough to keep the prize in sight. His admiration for the fish took on a hint of sympathy.

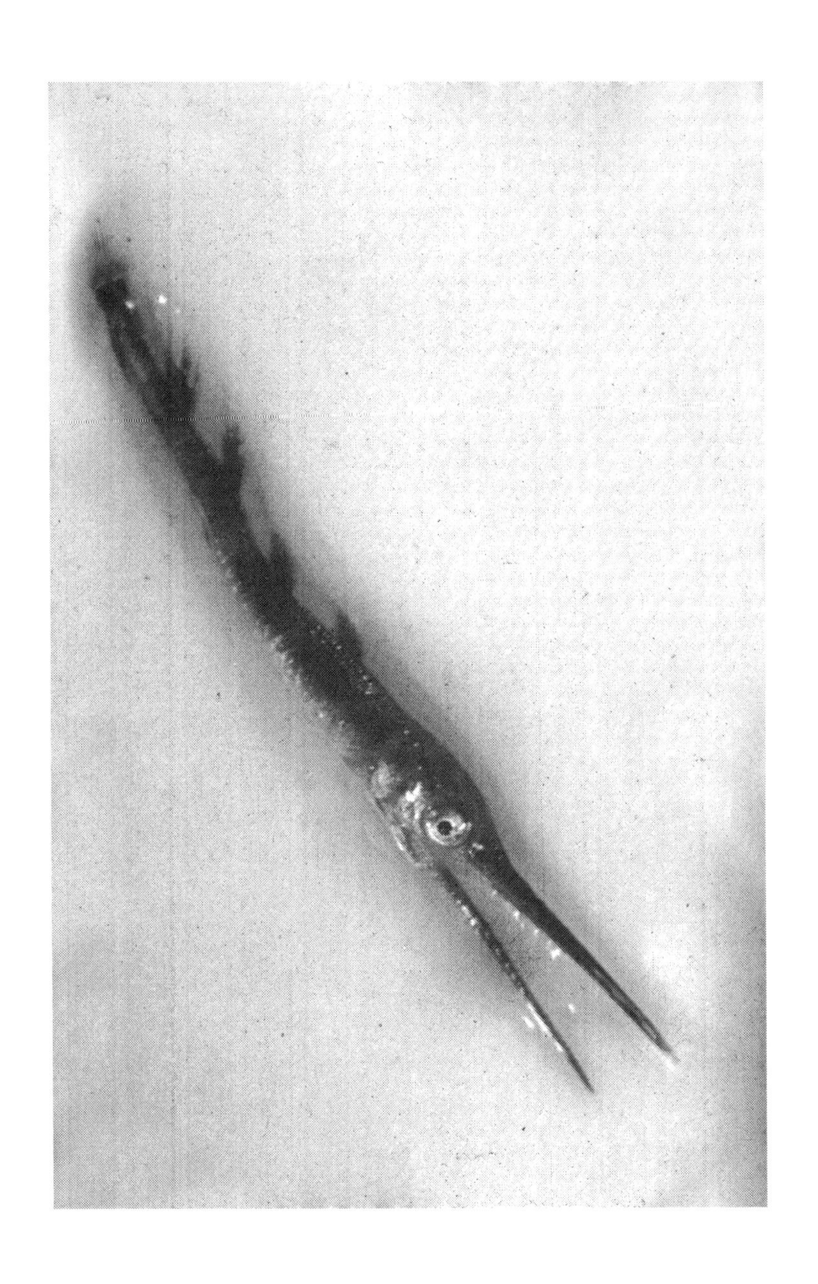

The Swordfish's Story

Eighty feet down, in the semi darkness, the big fish's five-foot tail beat slowly back and forth. With the four-and-a-half-inch bronze harpoon lilly buried at the base of her dorsal fin, she showed neither distress nor concern. An odyssey of a dozen years between Mexico's Yucatan Peninsula and Newfoundland's Grand Banks had hardened her into a seasoned warrior. She had seen a smaller fish live a healthy life with a 12-inch Greener rifle harpoon stuck in its back. She had also observed the rubber heel of a human shoe proudly skewered on a swordfish's bill with no ill effect. But now she only wanted only to get to the deep ocean where she would once again reign supreme, away from the threat of mako sharks, where this temporary annoyance would surely go away.

She had been conceived in the warm surface waters of the Gulf of Mexico. It was a haphazard affair that amounted to being abandoned with half a million other pinhead-sized eggs, their only protection a cloud of milt their mother's male companion had expelled in their direction. As the milt dispersed and visibility improved, hundreds of inch-long tunas and jacks swarmed the cloud of eggs, gulping down half of them before racing off after the prolific source.

The fertilized eggs that remained were nearly invisible. A small oil globule provided enough floatation to keep them in warm surface waters. Together, the globule and egg resembled a tiny contact lens, its transparency greatly reducing the chance of further predation. For half a day as the eggs dispersed in the ever-mixing surface waters no development was apparent. Then, when any observer's watchful eye would long since have glazed over, tiny stars of pigment began to appear, revealing a shape similar to every embryo ever conceived. Two startled eyes appeared on a pug-shaped face on one end of a shrimp-like body, whose tail tickled the owner's nose. In just three days the egg's development is complete.

A newly hatched larval swordfish must learn to swim so as to stay in warm surface waters after the egg yoke and oil globule are absorbed. For five days the hatchling is helpless, defenseless prey for any larger juvenile fish or carnivorous arrow worm that comes her way. But if she is lucky, she herself becomes a quarter-inch juvenile in just eight days after being abandoned by her mother. As yet no legendary bill graces the snout of this to-be predator. Instead she is equipped with a maw resembling that of a newly hatched robin.

How, one might ask, does a fish with the mouth of a newborn bird make a living in the open ocean with no mother to stuff it full of tender morsels? The easy solution would be to graze on succulent phytoplankton, but that wouldn't be in character for this aspiring apex predator. For ten days she pursues and devours flea-like zooplankton called copepods with a few chaetognaths thrown in. The copepod subsists on single-celled organisms including bacteria and diatoms. A chaetognath, or arrow worm, might dine on swordfish larvae for breakfast and become a juvenile swordfish's dinner. While this crunchy diet does not promote rapid growth in young swordfish, it does seem to contribute to the development of mandibles generously equipped with conical teeth. Soon comfortable with her formidable weaponry, the young predator abandons her diet of crispy critters and gorges on larval fish up to half her size. The change of diet prompts a 20-fold burst in her rate of growth that averages out to 50 pounds a year as she matures.

The Gulf of Mexico has all the ingredients for rapid larval growth. From the Yucatan channel comes wind-driven 78-degree

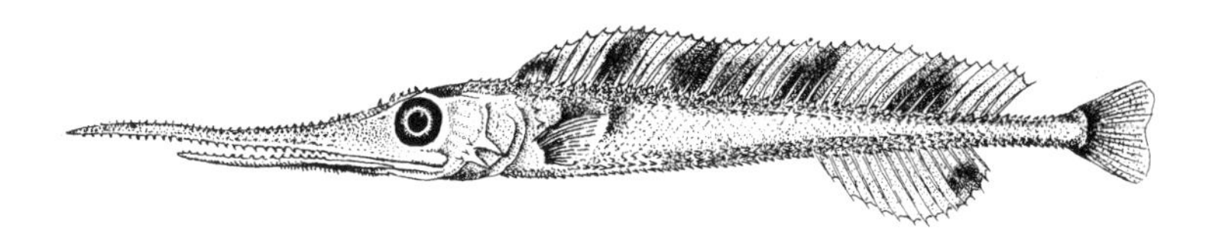

Atlantic surface water. From the north, continental drainage mixes with seawater in miles of estuaries, marshes, lagoons, and bays. The countless elements in these diverse waters create an explosion of biological activity that overflows from inlets and passes to waiting schools of ravenous finfish. While large areas of prolific swordfish spawning have been found in the tropical Atlantic, Caribbean, and Gulf Stream waters, nowhere but in the giant Petri dish that is the Gulf of Mexico is one likely to see juvenile dolphin keeping company with schools of mullet. The volumes of fresh and saltwater entering the Gulf vary with the season as do the currents that distribute these waters dictating the total volume that exits the Gulf through the straits of Florida. Thus the Gulf not only provides a productive environment that promotes the growth of juvenile swordfish, it also provides a stable sanctuary that allows advanced development before they are thrust into less nurturing waters.

Within the North Atlantic Ocean is a sea called Sargasso, named for the yellow "gulf-weed" that is actually a form of brown algae. Equipped with float bladders that allow it to drift on surface waters, most of the weed is torn from coral reefs by wave action; two species exist in the open ocean independent of land. Both collect at current and temperature edges providing cover for a large community of native residents and a host of aspiring apex predators looking for lunch. Young swordfish are nudged into this cornucopia by the same dynamics that collect the weed. They may start honing their newly acquired bill skills by dislodging small shrimp from the weed, reminding them of their copepod diet of their larval days. Next they might try to tackle a pipefish, the long snaky-looking relative of the seahorse. Eventually they will run up against the Sargassum fish itself. This frog-like fellow mimics the weed in which it lives and gulps down many that would share his shelter. The filefish, a small member of the triggerfish family, comes equipped with a dorsal spine and sandpaper skin, rendering it almost indestructible and hardly worth her trouble.

Our young swordfish soon tires of digging her supper out of the weed rafts. She flirts with the possibility of making a meal of the schools of swift swimming juvenile jacks and blue runners hiding from dolphinfish, wahoo and tuna in the shadows of the weed rafts, where they shared her menu. The jacks and runners can outswim her individually, but when they flee they run in schools and it doesn't take her long to learn that they don't see well at night. In fact, compared to her, they are almost blind at night! She quickly adopted a schedule of feasting on surface-dwellers at night and sinking into the twilight depths during the day to avoid the small-eyed predators that would be looking for her in surface waters.

As our young swordfish increased the depth of her dives, she became familiar with the layer of phytoplankton between the colder depths and the warmer surface waters. Like the canopy of a rain forest were nutrients and sunlight mix, this bloom of phytoplankton attracts a host of small but ravenous benthic grazers after dark. They, in turn, are hounded by equally voracious schools of squid, fish, crabs and shrimp. These schools create an electronic phenomenon known as the scattering layer for its depth recorder image. It migrates upwards to feast on phytoplankton during hours of darkness and descends into the depths with the coming of dawn. The swordfish developed an instant and enduring attachment to the scattering layer the first time she ate a squid. Not that there wasn't a plethora of other options. In fact, she ate twice as many mullet, quite a few viperfish and butterfish, as well as ribbonfish, moray eels, conger

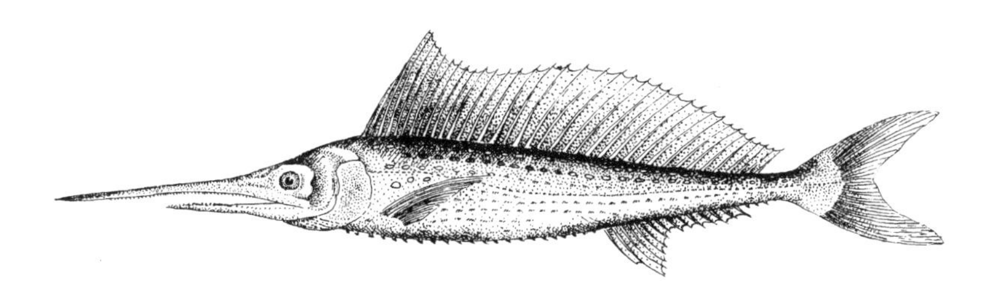

eels, snipe eels, and an occasional lobsterette. In addition, a smattering of herring, silver hake, blue runner, spadefish, octopus, tilefish, royal red shrimp, and even cat fish greased her chin. But it was squid that coaxed her east toward the Desoto Canyon. She watched as they zoomed in and out of the lights beneath a research submarine, grabbing the lantern fish that had collected there to feed on smaller prey. Soon she was in an area where squid made up most of her catch. She wouldn't pass up the occasional butterfish or tuna, but squid were thick, and seemed to be spawning any time they weren't eating. They were oblivious to their losses during their amorous activities. She was in Xiphias heaven.

In the spring of her third year she was on the edge of the shelf off Tampa. It was another good squid year and she was settling into her usual routine of nocturnal feasting when she became aware of a pungent oily scent. She moseyed into the current and rose slowly toward the surface to get a stronger sample. She heard clicking noises, first faintly and then more loudly. The sound grew louder, drowning out ambient noise. She dove slowly so that the "clickers" would not be between her and the depths when they met. Suddenly she broke into a southeasterly current and there they were: bullet-shaped, twice as big as she, hundreds of fish charging along with the current as if being pursued. Nothing our swordfish had ever met would challenge a gang like this. She assumed they were hurrying in the direction of a huge food source. The swordfish was quite content with her squid bonanza, but there was something about this teaming torrent of fish that piqued her curiosity. She found the depth of maximum favorable current and cruised south, dogging the endless column of bluefin tuna. No super source of food showed up, but at dusk on the second day of her adventure she came upon a knoll on the edge of the shelf south of Marathon, Florida, that teemed with blackfin tuna. She turned to stem the easterly current and waited for dark. Once dusk arrived to shrouded her approach, she slipped under the trailing edge of the resting school and started whacking the stragglers one by one. After the fourth kill, she had forty pounds of raw tuna to digest. She rose slowly to the warm surface waters and dozed as the Gulf Stream current swept her northeast along Florida's Miami coast.

During the night the bluefin tuna had veered east toward the Bahama side of the straits of Florida. At dawn our swordfish found herself alone as she sank into the depths. Reaching the ocean floor, she at once noticed parrotfish hiding in rugged outcroppings and golden tilefish nesting in holes in the soft bottom. These fish didn't tempt her as worthy dietary objectives. Soon however, she came upon other swordfish harassing these sedentary targets until they were dislodged, disabled and devoured. The bills of these fish had been gracefully sculpted by repeated contact with the limestone structure. While she found these activities amusing, she was not inclined to work quite so hard for a meal. Her patience was rewarded the next evening as she rounded an underwater promontory known as the Charleston Bump. Shoals of fish were stacked up in its eddy. She slipped into the countercurrent behind the lump. Holding her position, she eased up and down the water column, seeking the most vulnerable pod of fish. Yelloweye, red, and silk snapper, and a warsaw grouper meandered back and forth beneath a large nervous ball of cigar minnows. Wahoo and amberjack made blistering passes through the baitfish leaving scattered morsels to drift down to the waiting reef fish. It was the evening bite for small-eyed predators.

The swordfish's adipose fin twitched from side to side
ment. She coasted to the bottom to wait patiently for d

After an hour spreading terror in the "Bump" comı satisfied swordfish rejoined the Gulf Stream current and coasted northeast in warm surface water digesting her latest smorgasbord. Shelf waters along this stretch of coast supported a large shark population. She was not tempted to venture into the shallows. Three days after her latest kill, the current she rode accelerated. As she approached Diamond Shoals, she noticed school after school of baitfish stemming the current, feeding on larval shrimp flushed from North Carolina's mighty Pamlico Sound. The aggregation of prey was horizontal here as apposed to the vertical gathering at the "Bump."

The big fish coasted along observing a buildup of biomass resembling a seafood menu: hors d'oeuvres, small plate, seafood basket and "all you can eat." She mingled with apex predators that gathered 15 miles northeast of Cape Hatteras. In an area local fishermen call "the point," soundings dropped from 30 to 400 fathoms within a few miles. Here yellowfin and football bluefin took advantage of daylight to feed, as did blue and white marlin. As dusk approached, bigeye and albacore tuna became active. After dark the big swordfish joined other broad bills feasting on resting schools of skipjack and bonito that had found irresistible the endless current of bite-sized cannon fodder flowing from the Diamond Shoals. Excited by the competitive consumption she found it hard to quit. In fact she noticed that some swordfish continuing the kill without bothering to eat the remains of their attacks. Eventually she was stuffed and retired to digest latest meal. Meandering north in the warmest water she could find, the big fish became aware of a cool, rich smelling current she would eventually follow to the Grand Banks. But for the time being it was leading her to her next great discovery: Norfolk Canyon.

The eighteen canyons carved into the edge of the continental shelf between the Chesapeake Bay and peak of Georges Bank are

The work of 50 million cubic kilometers of glacial runoff mixed with tons of debris put in motion 15,000 years ago by rising temperatures. Each canyon has its own unique topography that results in dramatically varied marine populations and hydrographic characteristics. Steep increases in depth tighten the extremities of the life zones of the inhabitants of these prolific sanctuaries. Thus the predator that maxes out on tilefish at one depth need only drop fifty fathoms to feast on some unsuspecting redfish. Another kick or two from its massive tail finds it stirring up mud among the big-eyed rat-tails at the bottom of the canyon. To a swordfish "from away," New England's canyons are hybrid cathedral-supermarkets.

Like any tourist, the hungry fish makes a real pig of herself. Food was never more than a mile from sun-baked surface waters needed to digest the large amount of prey she was inhaling. And as she moseyed east into the new-found Labrador current, she could always find her fill of squid, but was not about to pass up a meal of whiting or a mass of juvenile haddock. By early November she had sampled the menu at every canyon west of Corsair and was amusing herself chasing huge halibut around their spawning grounds on the banks of the Northeast Channel. Her progress was interrupted by a three-day northwest gale. Water temperatures dropped to the low fifties increasing the distance between her food sources and water warm enough for digestion. She cruised southwest, planing up and down the water column in search of warm water. On one of her visits to the surface a small, black and white feathered missile shot by her, heading for the depths. As was her custom, she gave chase. She did not recognize the object's smell, so she ate it. Suffering no ill effects she spent the rest of the day picking off dovkies as they dove for krill in the cold surface waters on the southern edge of Georges Bank. This discovery did not solve her digestive requirement for warm water. After another day in bird-land she broke off the hunt and headed south for the warmth of the Gulf Stream.

She wasn't quite sure when it happened, but somewhere south of the Gulf Stream axis, a male swordfish started to shadow her. His presence disturbed her at first because it resembled mako shark behavior. Given the opportunity, a mako will sever a swordfish's tail at the caudal peduncle and dine on the helpless remains. It took her a while to give up the inclination to run off the shadow fish. After a few passes she began to admire his elusiveness and persistence. Running him off seemed out of the question. She finally accepted his companionship as long as she fed first and he protected her blind spot. By the time they returned to her familiar Gulf waters she realized her companion was an admirer. She did not take this event lightly as some male swordfish will follow the boat that harpoons its mate all the way back to port. Such were the hazards of the mating game. They would be mates for the next six years.

One flat calm summer day in her twelfth year, she was dozing west of the Nantucket Lightship digesting a catch of red hake she had taken in 35 fathoms of water. Her repose was interrupted by a small group of pilot fish that seemed to have lost its host and was considering her as a replacement. She was not pleased. They would be a distraction. She didn't need a pack of camp-following rudderfish flitting around while she was enjoying her afternoon nap. She took a couple of half-hearted swipes at them that should have been ample warning, but they simply scattered, regrouped, and circled around behind her. She leapt clear of the water, doing her best to land on them to scatter the school, but once again they found each other and made for her blind spot. She was about to make a lunch of pilot fish when she noticed the shadow and the hum of an engine close by.

Heading South

Lenny's dozing was interrupted as Tommy brought *Tecumseh* alongside the polyfloat. He idled the engine as Sammy gaffed the line leading to the orange ball. He lifted it gently to Franny who led the line through the rail-roller and backed herself behind an empty line tub. Sammy stowed the gaff and returned to the rail where he started the slow hand-over-hand haul that was least likely to startle the fish. Tommy threw the clutch in and out of idle, steering to keep the warp leading vertically from the water. Lenny was spellbound by the stealthy approach designed to bring to a successful conclusion a harpooning that had started with such wild abandon.

The sun was setting and the line tub almost full when the fish appeared from out of the deep. She was ironed through the base of the dorsal and slowly wagged her bill and tail in a weak swimming motion. Franny and Tom met at the landing gate, gaffs in hand. In unison they reached deep and gaffed the tail of the fish from opposite sides. They reared back but the tail of the fish was too wide to fit through the gate and too heavy to lift over the rail. She continued her slow thrashing. It was all they could do to keep her still enough for Sammy to reach around them with a hoisting eye opened a good five feet to get around the tips of the tail. Now it was Franny and Sam's turn to hold her tail with the hoisting eye as the gaffs were removed. Tommy put the cathead in gear, taking enough wraps to take the strain off the crew who were, by now, sitting on deck with their feet against the kick rail to keep from going over the side.

Slowly, the big fish inched up as the hydraulics groaned. The head appeared and Sammy cut her throat where the gills met. Purple blood poured down the side of the vessel. She moved no more.

Once the fish was aboard, Tommy called for Len to take the wheel as he headed *Tecumseh* south. Franny went forward to finish the evening meal, leaving instructions to save her the swordfish hearts. Sam and Tommy donned their foul weather pants, gathered hoses and knives and started cleaning the day's catch under glaring floodlights.

With difficulty they each rolled one of the big fish so that they were belly down, head toward the scuppers, thus lower than the tail. With a meat saw, they cut downward from a point behind the eye to the corner of the mouth. Sharp knives with rounded tips sliced forward from the upper corners of the gill plates to bisect the saw cut. Working with the fish on their sides, the two men cut along the collarbones to separate the head from the body. Other circular cuts were made to loosen the organs and free the membrane that separated them from the gut cavity. Straddling the carcasses so that the fish stayed belly up, they made incisions from between the pectorals to a finely carved circle around the vent. At this point, Sammy popped the air bladder and pushed the contents of the cavity forward. Tommy bubbled water from a deck hose into the cavity of his fish, then reached under the bladder to loosen it from its surroundings. Each man then took a firm grip on the lower jaw of his fish and with considerable effort, pulled head and entrails free from the body in one piece.

"Save the hearts," they reminded each other. Into a bucket of salt water went two dark purple organs the size of grapefruits.

After the gut cavities were sprayed and scraped several times to remove gobs of gelatinous slime, a 3-foot long rope of kidney was trimmed from the backbone. Generous scraping and scrubbing with rounded knife tip and stiff nylon brush removed all traces of kidney, leaving only a few flaps of loose skin and membrane to be trimmed.

Franny came on deck to claim her hearts and admire the two long chocolate colored carcasses that had by now lost all of their fearsome characteristics. To Lenny they looked more like Tootsie Rolls than gladiators of the deep.

"Big'un'll go six hun'rd pounds or more," Fran observed as she joined Lenny in the pilothouse. "She's got salmon-colored flesh. Must have spent some time in the Gulf of Mexico scarfing royal red shrimp."

"What are the grooves on their backs?" Lenny asked her.

"They're called corduroy. People say they're from diving deep to get food," Franny offered, "sort of like the grooves in a spongex float after it's been sunk for a while. Sperm whale have humongous washboard backs from diving deep for giant squid. They'll be gone when we take out at the end of the trip. Well, your supper's ready. Want to bag those hearts and put them in the ice chest when you go forward?" Franny took the wheel.

"Gotcha," Lenny replied. "We've been heading one ninety since we got the fish aboard."

"One ninety," repeated Franny as her gaze returned to the shapes on the darkening deck. They would go a long way toward covering the expenses for the trip.

After a supper of baked chicken, steamed carrots and rice, they returned to the floodlit deck. The day's catch was lowered to their icy berths and 500 mackerel from the broken boxes in the slaughter house were hoisted on deck. Five minutes after the deck lights went off, they were all in their bunk except Tommy, who cranked up all the radios in the pilothouse hoping to get some free information from a loose lip or two on the longline grounds several hours' steam away.

On the Longline Grounds

This was not Tommy's favorite part of the trip. He had started small, jig fishing cod inshore to avoid the structure of making a living on the hill. But, as resources diminished, gill netters had taken to leaving their nets in the jigging grounds between trips and when he moved to bottom trawls, starving draggers could not resist trying to share his catch by towing through his well-marked gear. He felt he had traded one straightjacket for another.

So Tommy had moved to deeper offshore waters. Following summer's finning swordfish to the edge of the shelf, he had floated halibut trawl with inflated auto tire inner tubes every five hooks. He spent that first night watching the flashing white blinker bulb over a radar reflector on the end buoy. It was a chilly, still, dark October night. They were outside the shipping lanes. Their only company was a display of northern lights that lasted until well after midnight.

The morning dawned glassy calm. The trawl arched toward the eastern horizon into a brass-colored ocean. Tommy followed the line of floats with his binoculars. Some lay quietly on the surface, others, in groups of two or three, were half submerged, nearly disappearing as gentle swells passed under them. The placid scene belied the turmoil beneath the surface. They hauled aboard four swordfish averaging 300 pounds before breakfast. Tommy carefully put harpoon holes in each fish before they went below. Better to pay the ten percent buyers took for the harpoon hole than have to do a bunch of explaining why he was buying all those tubes, line, and hooks.

The word got out soon enough after they lost the harpoon stand in a November gale and landed 60 fish without it. There was a brief honeymoon during which boats that already had trawl, fitted it with heavier leaders and hooks and spread out along the edge of the shelf. There was more than enough room for half a dozen boats. Talk on the radio was sociable, having to do with weather, water, and fish. Boats starting a trip would radio ahead to avoid other boats. Nobody wanted to waste precious fishing time unsnarling needlessly fouled gear. With the coming of spring and backordered gear, boats of every description flocked to the fishery, creating bedlam. It became another dog-eat-dog fishery. Tommy worked south ahead of the chaos. Reaching Norfolk Canyon at the end of May, he was only too happy to put his hooks ashore following the finning fish back north. July 4th found him harpooning south of Block Island. Working east, he finished the season on Brown's Bank by mid September.

He would occasionally switch from the spotter's channel to one of the longline channels around sundown when all the planes had made it ashore. What he heard made it a pleasure to be able to retreat to the forecastle for an evening of cribbage.

By the time the longliners had thinned out the shelf-bound harpoon fish, the Gulf Stream and a couple of hurricanes had thinned out the longliners. Tommy shipped the trawl gear back aboard. The boats that were left fishing relied heavily on information volunteered by the boats that had just completed trips. No longer would a good combination of temperature, depth, and bait guarantee a good catch. Tommy never stopped looking for "his own" fish. There were only a few owner-operated boats with whom he could share information without attracting a fleet of company boats. He didn't ask information of boats with which he didn't expect to share information. Company boats usually carried large crews. Company skippers rarely went on deck. This left them with a lot of time to listen and talk on the radio. Tommy had time to listen but little time to talk. Offshore obstacles had proliferated in the years since his first exploratory set. Lobster gear, red crab gear, even submarine-listening hydrophones crowded the edge of the shelf.

Tommy listened until he started to pick up lobster-gear reflectors on his radar. *Tecumseh* was approaching the edge of the continental shelf where the depth could drop 400 fathoms in less than a couple of miles. There was a "wall" of lobster gear between the 80- and 100-fathom depth contours. Currents generated by the dramatic submarine topography created cover and provided food to a large population of lobsters. Tommy picked up the VHF microphone.

"*Atlantic*, *Atlantic*, *Atlantic*; *Tecumseh*, You picking me up, Al?" Tommy knew Al was at the dock but there was a chance some boat with gear in the water within radio range would confirm what he already knew.

There was no comeback. Tommy switched on the autopilot and made his way forward. He took the tea kettle from the back of the stove. A couple of pumps of fresh water topped it off. He put the pot back on the front of the stove over the oil burner and gave the fuel valve a counter-clockwise twist. Franny stirred in her bunk, propped her head up with her hand and tried to focus on him.

"'Bout half an hour," he told her.

"And I was sleepin' so nice," she sighed, flopping back into her pillow.

Back in the pilothouse, Tommy watched the radar and steered to avoid one marker after another. The temperature, which had held steady at 66 degrees for the last hour, had begun to wobble up and down by half a degree. It was too late to look for a good temperature edge, and the lobster gear would dictate how deep they'd have to fish. He'd have to make a blind set, being as there was no one here, it would be a shame to miss a night running away from a possible spot with some wiggle room. He was drawing some comfort from having made his decision when a new target showed up one and a half miles outside the deepest lobster gear.

"Part off," he speculated, "not to mind." Then a second and third blip showed up each side of the first.

"Company," he groaned.

Franny and Len came on deck in hoodies, with slicker pants tucked under rubber bands at the ankles of their boots. Tommy turned on the deck lights and washdown hose. Lenny untied wash-tubs full of hooks and branch lines while Franny pulled the end of the mainline off the drum of the longline reel and passed it through the fair lead blocks to the setting table on the port side. Tommy was back on the VHF.

"*Breton Isle*, *Breton Isle*; *Tecumseh*, you got gear west of Veatch Canyon, Artie?" There was no reply. "Probably nursing a cool one with Al about now," Tommy thought.

Len put two tubs of gear side by side on the setting table while Franny filled a third tub on the table with pound-and-a-quarter mackerel. Sammy stopped by the pilothouse door with a 20-foot aluminum pole topped with a radar reflector on one end and two sash weights on the other. A polyball was shackled to the middle of the pole for flotation. At the same point, a 10-fathom branchline and stainless clip were fastened to attach the marker, known as a hyflyer, to the mainline.

"How we clipping, Cap?" Sammy wanted to know. Tommy thought for a moment, figuring where the wind would most likely be coming from in the morning and where the boat would be relative to the gear.

"We'll be going inboard, Sammy."

The branchline snap or clip is like a six-inch safety pin that grips the mainline in a notch rather than skewering it. The clip is opened by squeezing, and jamming it against the taut mainline. Removing clips is awkward if they must be pushed away rather than pulled toward the rail man who is unclipping the branch lines during the haul back. The gear is more easily retrieved jogging into the wind that slows the boat's progress enough to eliminate clutching the engine in and out of gear. It is also helpful to have the wind on the hauling side of the boat so it drifts off the gear in the water when pausing to handle a fish or snarl. To satisfy as many of these conditions as possible, gear set to windward was clipped inboard, gear set fair wind was clipped outboard.

Sammy lay the end hyflyer along the starboard rail and went to the pile of floats stacked behind the pilothouse to get half a dozen orange, basketball-sized buoys. Finally he took the eight-inch gutting knife from its holder on the rail and stroked a sharpening stone kept in a milk crate hung on the pilothouse.

Franny showed Len how to hook the mackerel: to drive the point of the hook down past the right side of the dorsal fin, into the gut cavity, under the backbone and back up on the left side of the fin to the rear of the original puncture. She then tossed the bait over the side several times to show him how to corral the uncoiling line between his hands and come up with the snap ready to clip on to the mainline. Lenny tried his hand. He smothered his first attempt trying to grab the clip.

"Let the clip come to you," Franny instructed. Lenny's second attempt flew into the dark when he missed the clip completely.

"That's better." Franny smiled. "Snub it with your left hand, then grab it and snap with your right." Lenny's third attempt was successful and he carefully coiled the branchline back in the tub.

"Don't you worry Len," Sammy helpfully volunteered, "you get snarled up, I'll cut you loose before you get drug over the side."

Franny shot a scowl of exasperation at Sammy.

"Just make sure everything is over the side before you clip to the mainline."

Tommy felt uneasy as he put a mile between *Tecumseh* and the radar targets astern. They were too perfectly spaced. The owner should be within radio range. This gear had not had time to get the least bit contorted by catch or contrary currents. He picked up the VHF mike.

"The boat with gear between Atlantis and Veatch Canyons, you picking me up, Cap?" Silence.

It was getting late. They'd had a long day. Tommy needed to get this set in the water. One last look at the radar put him a mile and a half outside the mystery gear. He leaned out the pilothouse door; "Let her go when you're ready, Sam ." Tommy brought *Tecumseh* to an easterly course as Sammy lifted the hyflyer over the rail and slid it into the darkness. Franny pulled on the mainline to get the winch spool turning up to the speed of the boat so that the gear would not be towed, resulting in twisted up branchlines. Sammy chucked a two-foot polyball and clipped the floatline to the mainline.

"It's all yours," he sang out to Franny. She waited for the vessel to travel a boat length before looping a bait to the edge of the darkness. A clip appeared to jump from the pile at the side of the tub opposite the hooks and slapped, as if magnetically, into the palm of her hand. She clipped it to the mainline that was now speeding astern.

"Number one," she said to herself, then "you're up" in Lenny's direction. "Number two," she prompted him as he finished clipping his first bait. When Lenny had clipped bait 10 to the mainline, Sammy stepped to the rail. He threw an 18-inch polyball on 10 fathoms of float line into the night and clipped it to the mainline.

"Ball one," he reported to Tommy. Nine floats, one hundred hooks, and a mile and a quarter later, Sammy slid a second hyflyer over the side.

Tommy watched the start of the second section of gear from the pilothouse, nudging the throttle forward as the crew on deck got into the rhythm of the set. The temperature had come up three degrees since they crossed the lobster gear but refused to budge since. Tommy would have looked for a cold edge inshore if he had any more room between his gear and his neighbor's. As it was, he had to steer a few degrees south of east to maintain a mile-and-a-half gap.

It was eleven-oclock when the last mackerel went over the side. Tommy took the engine out of gear and put on full right rudder to bring the gentle southwester abeam. Franny cut the mainline at a knot and tied a bowline in the end going over the side. Sammy clipped a two-foot polyball after the last hook and switched on a strobe light on the waiting end hyflyer. Fran handed the bowline to Lenny who clipped on the hyflyer floatline. Sammy waited until all the slack was out of the mainline then slipped the end buoy over the side.

In the time it took Tommy to fill out his logbook, the crew on deck had washed down the rails, deck, bait tubs, and setting table. Franny came to the pilothouse door.

"We're all finished on deck," she advised. "Going forward."

"Gotcha," replied Tommy without taking his head out of the radar hood. He didn't fool himself about obligatory sets like this one. Sets that he knew he made because he remembered taking fish under similar circumstances years ago, but with increased fishing pressure produced little now. It was these nostalgic flashbacks that kept him fishing. But for his own survival, he had to start training himself to ignore memory lane and go for the jugular like the younger set.

He pulled his head out of the hood, turned off the deck lights and looked for the strobe light. It winked at him from the darkness, the only other thing in sight. In the engine room Tommy pumped out the bilge and checked the propeller shaft stuffing box. Satisfied all was well, he turned off all but one light on the switchboard and headed up the ladder. Back in the pilothouse he switched the radar to the six-mile range and studied the last four radar reflectors on his gear.

"What's done is done," he mumbled; then switched to the 24-mile range and played with the gain looking for company. Finding none, he shut down the radar and engine. The whine of the antenna motor atop the pilothouse stopped and there was silence aboard.

Tommy started forward, then paused with his hands on the rail, searching the blackness to starboard until his eyes acclimated and he could start to pick out stars. A delicate loom was beginning to show where Lenny's moon searched for its place in the haze. He was thinking to himself what a soft, warm place the ocean could be and how rare these moments were on the surface where they had to work. For the fish below, it must be like this all the time, with only occasional voluntary trips to the surface in search of food or warmth. As he stood there, *Tecumseh* took a pronounced roll, sending the rub-rail down to give the ocean's surface a resounding kiss. Tommy headed below for a mug of hot chocolate.

Tecumseh meets the Phantom

An hour before sunrise Tommy's Westclock nagged him awake. He savored the warm comfort of his bunk for a moment, then remembered the phantom fisher whose gear he'd set next to. This brought him to a sitting position. He waved his feet around until he found his boots and lowered himself into them. On reaching the pilothouse, he opened the port door and scanned the southwest horizon with his binoculars: nothing. He put the radar on standby and went forward to wake Franny. The smell of frying hash met him at the doghouse. Returning to the pilothouse with his coffee, he dropped below to check the engine and clutch oil dip-sticks. Back in the pilothouse he started the engine and turned on the radar. The line of green blips on the display told him the story: he had drifted back into the lobster gear. Tommy put the engine in gear and leaned on the throttle. He steered south until he cleared the lobster gear. A maverick target showed up to the southwest. He switched on the autopilot, opened the starboard door and with one foot on the rail, searched the darkness ... a strobe light! He peered intently at the light trying to discredit his own observation.

"Mercy," he muttered and closed the door. Setting the autopilot southwest, he turned on the chart table light, plotted his Loran numbers and studied the chart. Inside the other guy's gear? He couldn't believe it, but if so, they were wrapped up; not the way you want to start a trip or meet a stranger. A row of targets began to appear on the radar. They were not perfectly spaced. There were occasional double targets and several sagging inshore of the rest. He groaned. As he approached his strobe flasher, he was further perplexed to see it being towed at half a knot offshore. He groped about for a less painful explanation. Could some big fish have sunk enough gear to anchor it up? He feared not. He lay *Tecumseh* to, shut down the engine and went forward for breakfast.

A hot plate of corned beef hash topped with two poached eggs awaited him on the stove. He poured a cup of orange juice and joined the rest of the crew already silently eating. Tommy didn't want to ruin anyone's breakfast with his suspicions regarding the gear, and he didn't want to say anything that would later suggest that he didn't know what was going on, so he too ate silently. Sammy finally broke the silence after a long thoughtful swallow of coffee.

"Did you hear what *Phalarope* ended up with yesterday?"

"Had four on deck when I last read 'em. He was on low power so I could only hear the plane working him after noon. Sounded like he could have had another four before they quit."

"Jeez, we ought to get a plane next year," Sammy ventured.

"I'd love to," Tommy mused, "but I'd have a hard time cutting a guy loose if the fish didn't show."

"If the fish are scarce *Hawk* could spot for two or three boats."

"Sammy, you harpoon for a full summer with all that time to eat and sleep and you'd be too fat to go on the stand," Franny chided. "They'd be winching you ashore with the fish by the end of summer!" She got up and started clearing the table.

Tommy joined her, pouring a cup of coffee from the pot on the stove. Adding cream and sugar from the table, he stirred the ingredients thoughtfully.

"We may be hung up on the phantom's gear for a bit," he said to no one in particular. "Ought to get started as soon as you're ready." With that, Tommy went up the ladder and disappeared into the half light.

Len looked from Franny to Sam for a clue as to what Tommy was talking about. Franny was the first to speak.

"Whoops!"

"Say it isn't so," sighed Sam.

The tide had slackened as they approached the flashing end buoy at dawn. Sammy hoisted the hyflyer aboard and stowed it in a rack along the starboard quarter. Franny unclipped his buoy line and made fast to the end of the mainline remaining on the winch. Lenny pulled enough mainline to reach the two-foot polyball that he hauled aboard. After coiling the float-line, he clipped it to the netting of the float cage aft on the port quarter. When Sammy was back to the rail-roller there came a hydraulic whine from the longline winch and the six-foot spool began to revolve.

Lenny marveled at the ease with which the line cut the smooth surface of the water as Tommy navigated from one float to the next. He could see untouched mackerel baits planing away from the boat as Sammy unsnapped the branch lines from the mainline. He held them back by the clip, stiff-armed, for Franny to pull out of his hand, never taking his eyes off the line ahead. Franny took the branchlines from him, put the clip in the far side of the tub on the coiling table and coiled the rest of the line, hand over hand, into the nearest part of the tub. Unhooking the still usable baits, she dropped them into a tub under the hauling table and put the empty hooks on the edge of the tub, starting at the handle closest to her. When they came to a float, Franny passed the floatline back for Lenny to haul.

"Gotta keep the clips separate," she instructed Lenny over her shoulder. "They can screw things up if they get into the coil pile."

The first five branchlines came in perfectly. The next five were wrapped up on the mainline in various degrees. Sammy grabbed for the dangling part of each wrap-up and pulled it off the mainline without stopping the winch.

"Line's being towed," Franny said, continuing Lenny's education. "Branchlines get parallel to the mainline and the baits spin up on it."

They hauled to the south until they reached the first of the phantom's gear: two large polyballs and a radar reflector on an aluminum pole floated with two big spongex floats.

"Red crab gear," Franny announced. "They fish just outside the lobster gear and they move every week to keep up production. They love to fish right at the depth we want to be in. Luckily there's only two of them."

Tommy stemmed the current next to the floats while Sammy and Franny worked to unwind a branchline that had spun around the bight of mainline that was hung up on the one-inch crab pot buoy line. Finally unsnarled, Tommy brought *Tecumseh* ahead until she was clear of the mooring. Then he turned hard to starboard, back toward the north, so Sammy could start hauling toward the next crab buoy. The wrap-ups ran away from the boat now, so they had to be hauled aboard, unsnapped and pulled off the mainline manually. It was slow repetitive work that promised few fish. It could also get dangerous around the moorings where the longline gear and hauler were no match for the heavier crab gear. Each hauling station was fitted with a knife in a holder under the rail but the knives came out only as a last resort.

They ended up with two small fish that day. Miniatures of yesterday's catch, they floated belly up as the *Tecumseh* approached.

"Hit the baits before the line hung up," Franny explained. "Died deep then floated when the current pulled them up and their air bladders didn't compensate." Once the gear was aboard and Tommy had headed east, Franny took Lenny aside and showed him how to find the knuckles that made it possible to cut off the fins and tail with the round-tipped slime knife.

"Some people use the meat saw, but it's not as clean as the knife and can leave sharp bony spines that tear up the other fish." She talked him through the cleaning of the first fish, then let him try his hand on the second. He had trouble circling the vent with his new Dexter knife.

"After you've done two or three hundred, your knife will thin down and make it easier," Franny promised. She showed him how to tell the difference between the reproductive organs attached to the vent. The female had two sausage-shaped ovaries that had a duct down the middle, the male had shoestring-like testes about eight inches long with a duct along the side.

"All the fish we harpoon are females," she said as much to herself as to Lenny. "Out here a quarter of the fish are guys. Three quarters of the fish are male in the Cuban fishery, could be a spawning thing."

Len managed to slice the lining of the gut cavity twice as he was scraping slime.

"Better than most," Franny observed. "We'll let you take that one home."

It was early afternoon as Lenny lowered the fish into the hold. Fran handed him eight boxes of bait and some ice to cover the second-hand baits from the day's haul.

They retired to the forecastle to find Sammy already snoozing. Fran put out sandwich makings, threw together a ham and cheese for Tommy and went up the ladder with a can of coke under her arm. When she returned, she sat across the table from Lenny, eating a sandwich of her own.

"Do we look for finners out here?" he asked after finishing his second sandwich.

"They seldom show out here," Franny replied. "Warm surface layer is thick enough so they don't have to horn out to warm up."

"Guess I should have gathered that," he said, motioning with his half full glass of milk toward Sammy's occupied bunk. "Is it safe to assume that we also have time for a kink?"

"Yah, Tommy's going to look long and carefully before he throws another set in the water." She yawned. "Last one asleep is a rotten egg."

Lenny slept soundly for three hours until his dreams started to become mini-flashbacks to his hitch on the proud cutter *Spencer*. His subconscious kept tapping his conscious on the shoulder until his eyes flashed open and he inhaled a long breath of pungent air. ECHO! he thought. He eyed his surroundings. He was still in his bunk aboard the longliner *Tecumseh* but all his olfactory senses put him at weather station ECHO half way between Bermuda and the Azores. He rolled out of his bunk. Franny was watching him with one half-opened eye.

"ECHO," he helpfully explained, and headed up the ladder.

He was greeted with warm tropical air so moist it was, at first, hard to breathe. The vessel was stopped in a calm sea full of patches of yellow Sargassum. Large cumulus clouds, some with showers falling from their lower edges, filled the sky. Tommy stood at the waist of the boat with a light spinning rod arched toward the horizon.

"You want to stand by with a gaff?" he asked, nodding toward the gaff rack along the rail.

Lenny grabbed a medium-length gaff and joined Tommy as a green and yellow fish, shaking off white water, jumped near a weed raft 50 yards away.

"Wearing him down, Lenny. Wearing him down. Now if his buddies don't cut him off trying to steal the jig, we've got supper makin's!" In their short acquaintance, Lenny had never seen Tommy show this level of emotion about anything. The captain seemed every bit as exited as the fish on the other end of the line.

"How long have you been 'wearing him down'?" Lenny asked.

"'Bout twenty minutes. Think I got the bull. If it wasn't for the rest of the school egging him on, I would have had him long ago." Tommy sounded something like a winter issue of the *Saltwater*

Sportsman magazine. "Wait 'til he comes by on his side," he instructed. "Don't show your gaff before that. When you go for him, go for the back of his head like you were shooting pool. That way you won't spook him. Sneak behind the line if you can so he doesn't get wrapped up and parted off if he jumps."

Lenny had a good ten minutes to sort out Tommy's string of suggestions. He liked the part about shooting pool and as the big fish made his third pass, Lenny lunged at him with the ferocity of the first break in tournament play. The results were similar. Water, instead of pool balls, went everywhere. Lenny was flattened against the rail. Tommy dropped the rod and grabbed for the butt of the gaff, hauling up to get the dolphin's tail clear of the water. Together they raised the walloping fish hand over hand to the top of the rail and between them to the deck where the slapping of his wet tail brought the rest of the crew on deck.

"Just in time for supper!" Franny cheered. Sammy grabbed the fish by the eye sockets and gave his nose a smart rap with a gaff handle. He knocked the jig loose with the heel of his hand. Tossing it to Tommy, he filleted the fish before its yellow sides with bright blue spots could turn silver. Lenny washed down with the deck bucket as Sammy arranged half the fish in a pan Franny provided.

"This place smells just like ocean station Echo," Lenny declared. Tommy was trying to tease another strike out of the now wary school. "We found a telephone pole floating out there that had a huge school of albacore living under it," he continued. "Filled every freezer on the ship before we ran out of gear. Captain called the pole a hazard to navigation and had us put a line and float on it so we could pass it to our relief cutter with instructions to hang on to it until we got back so no one would run into it."

"Smells like Echo because it is Echo, or a piece of it," Tommy said, skittering his jig across the surface of the water, challenging the dolphin to try to catch it. "The Gulf Stream gets meanders in it after it leaves Hatteras," he explained, making another cast. "If they break off the north side they become clockwise warm eddies moving southwest in the slope water. If they break off on the south side they become counterclockwise cold eddies and drift southwest in the Sargasso Sea." He paused to make another cast. "Some of the cold eddies run back into the stream and are reabsorbed." The school of seven fish followed the lure to the boat but did not strike. Instead of casting again, Tommy jigged the bucktail just above the surface but close enough so it popped the water like a wounded flying fish. This was more than the cautious dolphin could take and two of them dashed for the lead-headed lure. The first one grabbed it; the second tried to steal the head of the lure and parted Tommy off.

"One lure, one fish," proclaimed Tommy with satisfaction. "Help Sammy get up ten boxes of bait," he said as he headed for the pilothouse.

Once the bait was on deck with the box tops off so it would thaw, Lenny gazed at the pad of yellow weed that lined the side of the vessel. At first it seemed an empty mass of yellow floating in a bottomless sea of cobalt. That was striking enough. But as he watched, he saw first one, then another, small yellow shrimp flitting about avoiding small stalking crustaceans. They looked like baby blue crabs except they were ochre instead of olive. Then he picked out a pipefish slithering through the weed. On the bottom edges of the weed clumps were small schools of filefish and below them, nervous schools of small jacks. "Nervous for good reason," thought Lenny. Under the boat a school of larger jacks was gathering.

They sat down that evening to a meal of sautéed dolphin, coleslaw and rice with sword-heart giblet gravy. There was little talk until Sammy asked Franny for some more tartar sauce. While he waited for her to get it, he turned to Tommy, "So Cap'n, where is this place called Draconia?"

Tommy paused with his fork halfway to his mouth, "Never heard of it. You mean Laconia?"

"No, Angie and I'd been to a hill climb in Laconia. Got caught in the rain and crashed at some motel on 128. In the morning the lobby was full of people going to a meeting to decide the fate of the swordfish. Angie dragged me in. Said I could use the education. Some scientific type from Florida made a scary speech about fishing pressure. Then people in the audience started to make suggestions of how to save some fish for their kids. That's when the great Kahuna runnin' the show warned everyone not to panic and get all Draconian."

"Might he have meant that fundamentalist Greek dude who wanted everybody to wear a barbedwire bikini?" volunteered Lenny with a grin.

"It's management language for severe." Tommy finally made the connection. "Wiping out the sport and harpoon fisheries is OK but even talk of regulating longline effort, that's draconian. Woe is me!" He put the back of his hand to his forehead. "I used to go to those meetings until a guy I used to fish with was appointed to the council. He was a fair fisherman but he owned but one pair of socks. We'd try to grab a kink after bustin' ass all day and this guy would kick off his boots and the forecastle would turn green.

"Anyway, when he made council, I remembered what he used to say when we pleaded with him to set his socks with the gear. He'd say, 'You'll get used to it.' And that's just what his management attitude is to this day, no matter how bad things smell—'You'll get used to it.' That's the representation we got. Then they voted to join the International Commission of the Conservation of Atlantic Tunas to manage swordfish, which promised the same accountability that squandered the groundfish resource under the International Commission for Northwest Atlantic Fisheries. Well, that was the ballgame. I didn't have time to listen to them complain about what a bunch of overfishin' liars the 'furreners' were. There is no international enforcement. That's why they weaseled out of the domestic management to avoid any real accountability themselves. You're ruining my supper, Sammy."

"Sorry, Cap'. I didn't know we'd end up talking management." They concentrated on fishing for every other waking hour. Tommy liked to take time-out at mealtimes.

That evening they set out at dusk in a glassy calm. The deck lights penetrated deep into the navy blue ocean. Patches of Sargasso weed lay suspended like clouds of gold. The temperature edge had pushed up onto the bank where Tommy could not follow it. Instead he stayed on the 300-fathom contour heading east in 76-degree water. He knew he should have steamed directly to the temperature edge at the east side of the eddy. But he couldn't resist sampling the core of the gyre that might yield some tunas not included in the usual swordfish set. They set past two huge, floating tree stumps with roots clawing the air. Sammy adroitly threw floats over the shaggy thickets, quickly clipping the floatlines to the mainline.

"Tuna country," he whispered in Lenny's ear. "Spit on them baits, Boy. We're in tuna country."

Impressed with his own marksmanship on the tree stumps Sammy started dribbling the floats around the deck before launching game-tying hook shots into the darkness at float time. He was Bob Cousy for one section of gear, then John Havlicek for the next. He did the give-and-take with Bill Russell, who was the side of the pilothouse, and dribbled up behind Lenny. "It looks like the kid has the ball on a string," he announced in his best Howard Cosell impression.

Lenny concentrated on the hook count. They were out of bait after extending the 12th section with two additional floats. He felt he'd been longlining his whole life. Quickly they washed down the deck, rails and setting table. Tying down the empty branchline tubs, they took off their foul weather gear and headed below. All three were in their bunks when Tommy arrived to make himself a hot chocolate. He'd take the first watch to establish *Tecumseh*'s drift relative to the end buoy. If he had to steam back to the buoy before his two-hour watch was up, he would know the time and direction his relief would have to steam to keep up with the buoy's progress. He would call Sammy in two hours, who would call Lenny, who would call Fran, who would be getting breakfast at the end of her watch. Everyone would get six hours sleep.

The next morning dawned gin clear with a cool zephyr coming off the bank to the north, where a thick fog hung over the colder water. The sun was already warming their backs as they started hauling back toward the west. Three medium-sized yellowfin tuna livened up first section. They must have been hooked at dawn. The three fish were trying to sound and had half-submerged the floats either side of them. As they came in sight under the boat they swam in circles. Sammy unsnapped each branchline and handed it to Franny who snapped it to the eye in the end of a length of line coiled in a five-gallon bucket under the hauling table. This gave her some slack if the fish made a run she couldn't stop. Lenny stood by with the long gaff reciting Tommy's instructions from the day before. Eventually the fish would run out of room to circle and break the surface.

"Now, behind the eye," Franny wheezed between clenched teeth.

After Lenny struck, the solid fish never stopped struggling for a moment. It was either turn the fish or lose the gaff and Lenny was not about to lose the gaff. He heaved back and the fish ran into the side of the boat. Sammy, coming from nowhere, sank a hand gaff into the back of the fish's head. Together they towed the fish to the gate and lifted it aboard. Again and again Sammy's well-placed gaff paralyzed a fish and as Lenny freed his gaff, Franny cut the tuna's throat, releasing jets of purple blood. Sammy dragged each fish to a pen where the deck hose would start the cooling process.

The next section was not as successful. Sometime during the night a trunkback turtle the size of a VW had run into a branchline. The hook at the end of the branchline had looped around its flipper and caught on the leader making a lasso that held the monster fast as long as it struggled, and struggle it did. It was all Lenny and Sammy could do to haul the flipper high enough for Franny to get a hand gaff through the bend of the hook.

"I've got it!" she finally grunted and as the line went slack the loop opened and the turtle was freed. It lay there very still by the side of the boat as if trying to decide whether or not to thank its tormentors. Slowly a head the size of a bowling ball emerged from between its flippers and broke the surface. Heaving a great sigh, it took one last look at the spell-bound audience lining the rail, and smoothly dove out of sight.

As they hauled into warmer water a school of dolphin started to follow their progress. They were too small to swallow the mackerel baits but would feed on the particles shed from broken baits. They quickly learned to race each other to each successive float beneath which schools of small jacks had gathered for shelter. As Lenny pulled the floats from the water a small feeding frenzy would ensue. He felt sorry for the jacks. Some made it to the hull of *Tecumseh* to join a growing school of survivors.

Further down the line Lenny heard Sammy warning Franny, "Stingray, Fran; heads up!" Franny cautiously swung a black, flapping bat-like ray over the rail. Carefully she carried the squirming catch to the gate where she got a hand gaff in the bend of the hook. Holding the stingray over the side she gave a quick jerk and it splashed harmlessly back into the sea.

"That, ma boy, is one bad dude," she observed. "Some Japanese fisherman flipped one aboard and got the spine in the chest. Killed him."

As they drew close to where the first of Sammy's stumps should have been, the line took a turn to the south. Two hyflyers could be seen ahead within a hundred yards of each other.

"Think you might have hooked Bill Russell?" Franny wondered out loud. They started getting wrap-ups as they approached each float. Clearly the line had been towed. At the middle of the section they hauled aboard three dead 150-pound bigeye tuna that had taken adjacent baits and headed for Bermuda. Hauling back to the north they had turned west again when they approached another two hyflyers. This detour was not as simple as the first. The two parts of the bight of line towed south had been married and twisted into an inseparable macrame. Sammy and Lenny hauled the tangled mess into empty tubs while Franny pulled off any branchlines or float lines she could quickly salvage without slowing the already tedious process. Gradually they neared the cause of the wrap-up, whatever it was was still strong enough to swim circles around the *Tecumseh.* They had long since buoyed off and left behind the remaining undisturbed line leading west, so Tommy was able to turn the boat to keep the mystery critter abeam. Now a pointed black fin occasionally broke the surface. Lenny then Fran joined Sammy hauling the snarl. By this time the branchlines could not be removed, so the hooks had to be cut away as they hauled, otherwise someone could be hooked and dragged over the side if they started to lose the tug-o-war. Eventually two fins started to clip the surface side by side, some 12 feet apart.

"There's two of them!" blurted Lenny.

"Nope, grunt, only one, grunt, one big mother of a Devilfish," Sammy panted.

"Manta ray, harmless but huge," added Franny.

The ray finally let them haul it to the gate. It had done a dozen back somersaults, wrapping the mainline between its horns and around the back of its fins. Tommy came to help hold the lines as Sammy hung over the rail with a ripper trying to cut the ray loose. The exhausted animal was struggling to breathe but its gill vents were pressed against the side of the boat causing buckets of water to spit into Sammy's face. He finally cut the last restraining turn of line and the great animal flipped effortlessly on its back, flying out of sight under the hull of the boat.

"We just cut loose half a trip of skate wing scallops," reflected Sammy, hauling aboard the last of the tangle. "Looks like we'll be busy enough unwinding snarls without bagging bivalves."

"I had a platter of those sweeties in Morehead City once," Franny piped up. "Dam'd if they didn't taste better than the real thing! And they didn't even punch them out in circles; just whacked them up every which way. Might have been tongues and cheeks to look at 'em. But, Oh Boy, were they yummy. I might slap my grandma for another mess of skatewing scallops!"

They returned to the cut-off end on the line and started hauling the last two sections of gear before the first billfish of the day finally showed up. Even then, it arrived in the form of what Sammy called a "skilligalee."

"White marlin to you, Lenny," Franny said, as she showed him how to hold the elliptical bill with her left hand and knock the hook from the corner of the fish's mouth with the heel of her right. Tommy was leaning over her at that moment holding a three-foot pole that he used to bury a miniature harpoon into the back of the marlin. Trailing from the little harpoon was a six-inch yellow piece of plastic spaghetti with writing and a number on it. Franny gave the fish a gentle pull through the water and released it. Three hooks later another white came alongside that Len got to release.

"Lucky suckers get to spend winters in Venezuela," explained Franny. "We've gotten two returns from there in the last two years. They'll be out of here with the first autumn northwester. Smart animals."

The last section produced two swordfish, each weighing less than a hundred pounds. "Should have stayed inside with Eddie and *Hawkeye*," Sammy lamented as they cleaned the catch. Tommy

turned *Tecumseh* to the east as the crew put eight fish below and went forward for lunch.

Franny took Tommy's meal aft to the pilothouse, then attacked the snarl pile with Sammy and Len. First they stripped the branchlines and floatlines from the tangled heap. Then each found or made a bitter end by cutting the mainline at a knot and started pulling, coiling and dipping their piece of line through the pile until they came to one another or another knot. Untangled coils were joined together into empty tubs ready to be coiled back on the winch spool. Once the floats and floatlines were reunited and stowed, the crew repaired the cut and parted branchlines. These were half braided nylon and half monofilament nylon, fastened together by a loop connection. Franny showed Len how to tie the hook knot once new mono was attached to the braid. She sat on a milk crate in front of a ring welded to a rail stanchion. Taking the hook by the shank in her left hand, she licked the end of the nylon and put it through the eye of the hook twice. Then she wrapped the same end clockwise, around the standing part of the nylon three times and tucked it, away from her, through the wraps made previously around the eye. Grabbing the end of the mono with her teeth, she slowly pulled the slack from the knot so that it was settled enough to put in the rail ring. There, with the rest of the leader wrapped around her butt, she pushed off with her feet to tighten the knot permanently. She showed Lenny how, when tied correctly, the end of the mono pointed away from her hand when the hook was held in the baiting position.

"Nothing worse than getting that sharp nylon spike hung up in your glove while you're trying to get rid of a bait," she declared. While Lenny practiced the hook knot, Sam and Franny finished the branchlines and ran seven tubs of recovered line back on the winch. At five in the evening, Franny went down forward to start supper. Lenny and Sam got up 15 boxes of bait and turned in for a short power nap.

Tommy found the east edge of the eddy before supper and turned in toward the bank. To his surprise there seemed to be no one in the area. He followed the weed line of mixed rock weed and Sargasso weed to the 200-fathom curve where the moisture-laden eddy air turned to fog over the colder shelf water. He was still a mile from the lobster gear. He decided to lay-to during supper to get an estimate of the drift. He felt good about this spot. The productivity from the mixing of shelf and slope waters along the drop-off always attracted predator fishes. Tommy would spend the first night along the temperature edge, locating the seam of peak productivity.

Franny had made a pork chop casserole for supper. Peppers, onions and celery smothered with mushroom soup had steamed over eight chops that had, with the help of some chicken stock, marinated over a layer of rice. The results, with some applesauce, made for a quiet dinner table. Tommy was first to finish, put his plate in the sink and poured himself a cup of coffee.

"You might get up another two boxes of bait before we get started," he said to no one in particular and went up the ladder. Sammy smiled at Franny.

"That's good, right?" asked Len.

"That's real good," answered Sammy starting on the dishes.

Tommy moseyed to the west along the 300 hundred-fathom curve as the deck was readied for setting. They had drifted offshore during supper. The water warmed to 76 degrees in a few minutes. That was as high as he had seen it all afternoon. He planned to turn east then south, cooling off about a degree a section for 15 sections. When the baits sank to the point where they collided with the more placid cold water, the line would tend to anchor on the temperature edge separating the cold water, where the fish fed, from the warm water, where they would go to rest. Tomorrow Tommy would know at which surface temperature his gear would be most productive.

The set went off flawlessly. They started east in the clear azure eddy water that turned black as they approached the weed line at section eight. Tommy stayed on the weed edge for a couple of sections then started easing east, looking for the end of the tongue of cold shelf water he expected to be hugging the east edge of the eddy. The water started to cool fast to 66 degrees and turned cloudy green. He turned *Tecumseh* back to the south and then went west for the last section in clear dark green water, the looks of which Tommy liked a lot.

The deck was empty by the time Tommy had finished filling out his logbook. He turned off the deck lights and looked for the strobe that winked at him from the port quarter. Below the crew was finishing off dishes of pound cake, strawberries and whipped cream. Tommy joined them and poured some coffee before returning to the pilothouse for the first watch.

A Hazard to Navigation

Lenny was sleeping soundly when Sammy gently shook him. "I've got a hazard to navigation out here, Coastie, can you give me a hand?" Lenny slipped into his boots and followed Sammy up the ladder. Sammy made his way to the gate in the rail that was already open. He was taking off his T-shirt and kicking off his boots and socks as Lenny caught up with him. He handed Lenny a polyfloat and snapped the floatline to a belt loop on the back of his pants.

"Haul me back when I reach the end of the line," Sammy ordered, and without another word, he slipped into the water and pushed off from the side of the boat. He did a tankerman's breaststroke through a pan of Sargasso weed illuminated by the range light. It was the same stroke Lenny had learned in boot camp to be used in case he ever had to swim through burning oil. As Sammy approached the outer edge of the weed, Lenny could make out a shiny black object. Sammy wrapped his arms around it. Slowly Len retrieved Sammy and his mysterious catch. Santos slithered, otter-like, back aboard.

"Give me a hand," he whispered. They reached over the side together and hauled aboard a surprisingly light, plastic covered cube that measured two feet to a side. As they sat down, the duct-taped bundle landed on them and Lenny recognized the object for what it was. He tried to stifle a giggle. Sammy helped him with one hand over Lenny's mouth and the other on the scruff of his neck. He spoke softly in Hill's ear.

"I dove eight summers for nickels off MacMillan Pier to keep my Daddy drunk. This here is my payday. Now you go forward and get a quiet cup a Joe and I'll see you in the wheelhouse." Lenny nodded his complete agreement with these simple instructions. Sammy slowly released him.

They met in the pilothouse five minutes later. The only sign of their adventure was Sammy's damp pants; the cuffs were outside his boots rather than inside where they belonged. Sammy casually pointed out the strobe flasher winking off the port quarter.

"Captain steamed up on the end buoy at midnight but she's settled down since then. You'll make it to Fran's watch easy." He patted Len on the shoulder. "Have a good one, see you in the morning." Picking up his coffee cup he headed out the door leaving Lenny no chance to make further conversation.

Lenny took a swallow of his coffee and climbed into the pilot chair, resting his feet between the spokes of the ship's wheel. He leaned back and scanned the blackness from beam to beam with the 7 by 50s. His thoughts wandered back to the nut-brown swimmers that he had watched treading the clear green waters of Provincetown harbor when the *Spencer* would call there to pick up fisheries observers. It had never occurred to him that these boys would have to grow up and leave a pastime at which they excelled and which seemed to be such great fun. They would taunt the tourists with good-natured insults to encourage generosity with the coins the boys knew they carried. Nor had it ever occurred to Lenny that these urchins were not always as happy as they appeared in the water.

Watching them and smelling that pier reeking with the aroma of creosote and sun-baked oil of mackerel, it was easy to forget winter and the more serious business of survival the other nine months of the year. Lenny was sure the boys could have snatched most of the coins out of the air before they hit the water but there seemed to be an unspoken code that this would discourage business. So they always let the coins hit the water, which made a graceful, competitive dive necessary. Teamwork, competitive exercise, psychology and an income, thought Len, not a bad curriculum for an informal summer school.

By morning, the shelf water tongue had encroached on the east end of the set sending the surface temperature down to 62 degrees. They caught several savage-looking handsaw fish with catlike eyes, transparent teeth and long snaky bodies whose sides shone like mother of pearl. For all their ferocious appearance, their entire diet seemed to be helpless comb jellies that they immediately disgorged when picked up by the tail. Next, the crew tussled with three 7-foot bluedog sharks. After being hauled to the rail, they were handed off to Tommy, who tucked his feet under the bottom step leading to the pilothouse and leaned over the rail. With a double wrap of the leader on his left hand, he carved free the hook in the corner of each shark's mouth.

The most colorful catch of the day was a 3-foot-long fish Sammy called a "Madeira turkey." Deep-bodied, and Day-Glow orange, it was sprinkled with spots the size and color of a silver dollar. Sammy's father had fished for opah from the island that made the wine, during the seagoing saga that brought him ultimately to America on the deck of a whaler. He had easily found replacement for the island wine but a dearth of his favorite fish. Sammy gilled and gutted the fish between floats while Franny and Len continued to haul. The next time Lenny looked at the opah only the fins were orange. While the dots remained white, the body had turned gray.

Hauling out of the cold water, the line made a turn to the south in 68-degree surface temperature. The swordfish started to come as if punched out by a cookie cutter: one 125-pounder after another. They had only had six sections in the seam but ended up with thirty fish. That pleased everyone except Sammy who was hoping for another opah.

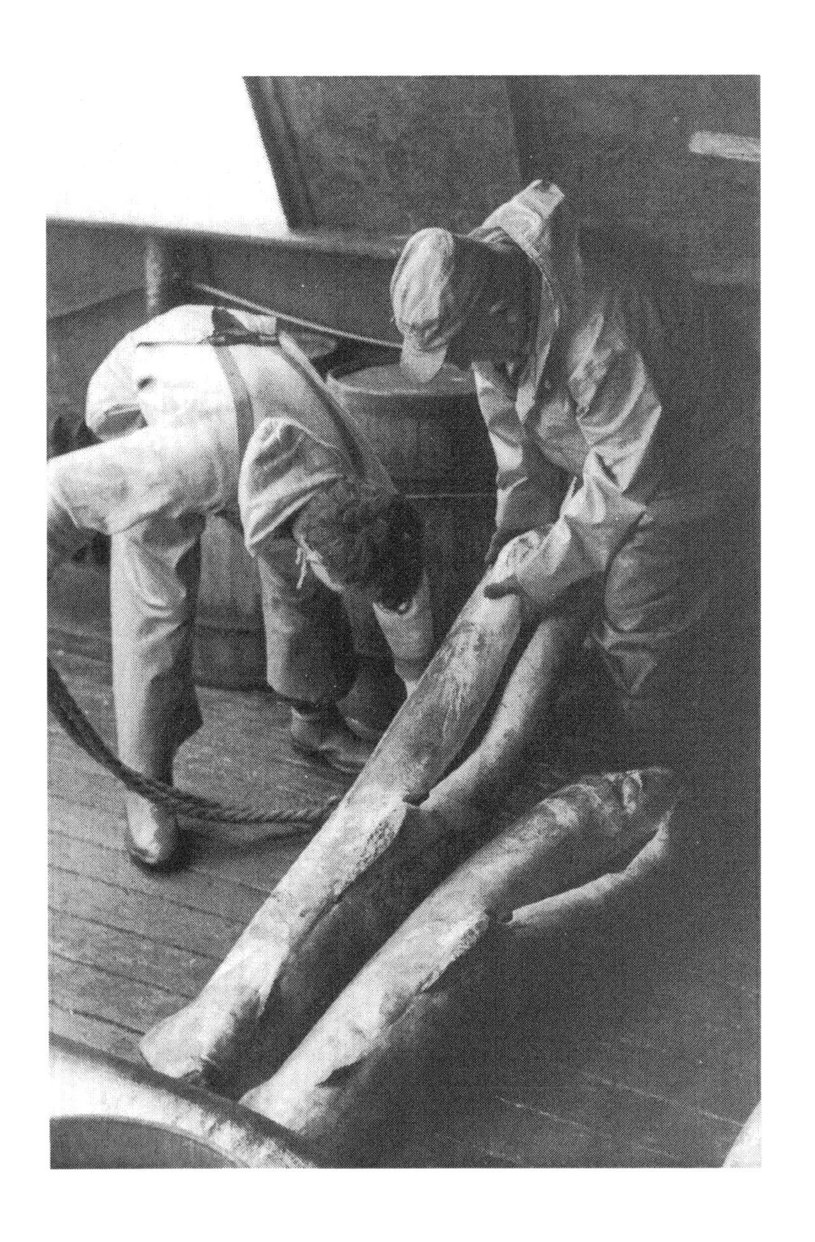

Packing the Catch

Tommy steamed for the bank while the crew went below for a quick lunch before starting to clean the day's catch. By the time Tommy neared the haze marking the bank, Fran and Sammy had gone into the hold to chop ice and prepare a pen for the catch, while Lenny finished scrubbing his fourth fish. Tommy lay *Tecumseh* to and showed Lenny how to strap the cleaned fish waiting to be hoisted into the hold. The straps were six-foot loops of line whose strands had been untwisted, then braided, to make them wider and softer than normal line in order to lift the fish without bruising their flesh. Tommy lay the loop strap next to the fish and rolled the carcass over it in such a way as to have the end of the strap just forward of the fish's vent. Then he pulled the rest of the strap through the eye and tightened it over the belly cavity. This positioned the strap close to the balancing point of the fish so they could be sent down the hatch head or tail first depending on the instructions from the packing crew below.

Tommy and Len strapped the six largest fish and waited for the word to lower them. Tommy then manned the cathead, lifting the fish off the deck while Len guided them over the hatch and down to Sam, who slid them across the ice to Franny, who unhooked the strap. Taking the hoisting eye out of the bight, she hooked it up to the hoist again so Len could pull the strap from under the fish. Franny held the gut cavity of each fish open so Sammy could shovel it full of ice. Once Lenny got the hang of it, the four of them were in continual motion until the last fish was iced and they took up bait for the evening set.

Everyone got an hour's rest before dinner. Even Franny flaked out after putting a meat loaf, candied parsnips and baked potatoes in the oven. The anticipation at the supper table was palpable. They'd had a good sign of fish. Each was extrapolating the number of days it would take at today's catch rate to fill the boat. Sammy found it difficult to contain himself when they were doing well and would circumvent Tommy's fish talk prohibition by making thinly veiled statements that required no conversation.

"Eat hearty, Len, we want you keeping up with the dressing crew tomorrow."

"Fran, I got half a mind to throw away all the old bait and give them nothin' but fresh tonight."

And as Tom put his plate in the sink and poured his coffee, Sammy observed: "Bet old Eddie *Phalarope* would trade places with us tonight."

"I'll be ready when you guys are," Tommy said as he went up the ladder.

Steaming north, Tommy lowered the temperature to 68 degrees, then headed northwest to find where the temperature intersected the 200-fathom contour. As they approached the edge of the bank, the visibility diminished with the heat of the day. A line of lobster gear inshore was the only target on radar. Tommy turned southeast as the fathometer edged up to 200, Sammy slid the end buoy over the side and they were off on set four of the trip. Two and a half hours and 1,500 hooks later, Sammy slid the strobe light buoy over the side and gave a "thumbs up" sign to Tommy.

The pressure of finding fish was gone. They could sit around the galley table sipping their hot chocolate, making small talk, knowing at this moment they were the envy of everyone they knew. In their minds they were sharpening their wits to take full advantage

of this opportunity. In their dreams they saw bobbing polyballs being towed to and fro.

They ate breakfast before dawn and idled up to the end buoy flasher in the half-light. Within the arc of the deck lights they could see several half-submerged floats. They hauled three fish aboard before reaching the first float. Sammy called them "flasher fish" because they seemed to be attracted to the strobe light. They had a few snarls resulting from the slack line at the end of the set. Once they hauled into the second section, the fish came like clockwork, one after another every ten or twelve hooks. There was little time for banter but Sammy let it be known he was rooting for a fish for every float they used; a roundabout way of predicting 150 fish. As it turned out, they were only eight fish shy of that when they finished hauling at 11:30. The fish were piled rail high on the port side giving *Tecumseh* a decided list. Big fish that could not be stacked, crowded across the front of the pilothouse from rail to rail.

After a 20-minute lunch break, they went silently about the ritual of cleaning the catch. A flock of shearwaters gathered around the port scuppers to squabble over the discarded refuse. Sammy called them "New Jersey birds" because they started every sentence with "Yeah!" Once the large fish were dressed and below, they had enough room to work up the pile of smaller individuals. Tommy was on his knees removing the kidney from a 100-pounder when Sammy, who was straightening his back between fish, remarked, "Oh shit. Don't look now, but here comes one of those near-sighted, absentee owner, Clorox bottles, sportin' a set of crutches."

Tommy kept trimming kidney while he translated Sammy's observation: a company-owned, fiberglass St. Augustine trawler, with the pilothouse forward, dragging flopper stoppers from the outriggers that were originally used to tow shrimp nets in her home waters. Tommy stood to get a hose and scrub brush to finish his fish. Observing the approaching vessel he noted without elation that Sammy had scored four out of five correctly. The converted shrimper looked more like a Desco trawler.

It was too late to lead the newcomer off his spot. The flock of shearwaters gave away the fact they had fish and it was too late to get them below. They were caught. Tommy kicked himself for not having steamed into the gear on the edge of the bank to imitate a lobsterman. At least they had gotten the large fish out of sight.

The crew of the *Tecumseh* kept cleaning fish as the shrimper, *Cap'n Fitz*, idled to within 50 feet to give the crew hanging over the bow a good look at the activity they hoped soon to join. "How many head chall figga ya killed?" called one of the newcomers. Tommy stood and surveyed the deck from bow to stern as though giving the request serious consideration. "Think we'll end up puttin' a generous 50 down," he allowed, and went back to cleaning his fish to discourage further interrogation. One by one the audience on the bow of the shrimper diminished and the skipper, hanging out the pilothouse window, pointed skyward as he put the Caterpillar in gear and idled away. Tommy sighed, took off his gloves and washed his hands. *Cap'n Fitz* wanted to talk.

After the usual formalities it became obvious to Tommy that the skipper of the *Cap'n Fitz* wanted to share his life story with everyone within radio range and find out how Tommy was catching his fish without actually asking. His technique was to feed Tommy several minutes of worthless historic information and hope Tommy would update it with useful current facts. Tommy had learned early on that skippers of absentee owner boats had very short memories. Now he gave them only what they had to offer, which was usually nothing.

After a few minutes the conversation got decidedly one-sided and Tommy could come on deck and clean a fish between transmissions. Finally it was dinnertime on the *Cap'n Fitz* and Tommy signed off having told the skipper only that *Tecumseh* was going to set that evening in 70-degree water. Tommy hoped the southern skipper would favor the warmer water just as Tommy had a few nights before. If the *Fitz* respected his 70-degree berth he would have two miles wiggle room. If he didn't, it would be more like a mile and a half.

Lenny helped Sam pack the fish below while Fran gave Tommy a hand on deck lowering the fish. They were washing down after taking the bait up when the *Cap'n Fitz* dumped a buoy southwest of them and started setting gear to the southeast. "He's going to make a lot of sharks very happy before the swordfish start to bite," mused Sammy. "Greed doesn't pay."

They had a leisurely dinner of broiled lamb chops, mint jelly, peas and steamed new red potatoes. Tom sat with Sam and Franny for a cup of coffee while Lenny did the dishes. They talked about the Red Sox losing the pennant again, but they were thinking about the trip that was almost theirs.

Tommy steamed to the bank as the crew set up the deck. He eased a bit east to anchor the north end of the gear in 66-degree water. Turning south, Sammy waited for his signal and dropped the end buoy for set five. With one section of gear in the water, Tommy picked up the *Fitz's* end buoy at three miles on his radar. "Oh good," he thought. "At least he started in 70 degrees." Tommy got to 68 and turned southeast. He could see a flasher on *Fitz*'s north end buoy. By the fifth section Tommy could pick up seven of *Fitz*'s radar reflectors. They were slowly converging on *Tecumseh*'s course. "Covering the waterfront just a little bit," he said to himself. As they set the tenth section, the two strings of gear were still two miles apart. Tommy knew he was home free. The warmer water was going to sweep the *Fitz*'s gear away from his. They had survived round one with the competition.

It was a little after 2A.M. when Sam woke Lenny for his watch. Len thought it a little unusual that the engine was running. When he got on deck he noticed a flashing buoy close aboard but it was an incandescent flasher and not their strobe. Sammy greeted him at the pilothouse door. "I need you to hold on to something for a minute," he said, pointing at the nearby buoy. Lenny knew better than ask questions and went forward to grab the flashing radar buoy as Sammy nudged *Tecumseh* alongside and came forward with a fat plastic bread bag, its end lashed closed with twine. He put a rolling hitch on the hyflyer staff Lenny was holding and tied off the loose ends with a square knot. "There now," he said to Lenny. "Let'er go."

Back in the pilothouse Sammy put the engine in gear and eased the wheel to starboard. There was a cough from the chart room behind them as they slid away from the flasher. Sammy steadied up *Tecumseh* in a southeasterly direction and pointed ahead until Lenny made out a strobe light winking some three miles away. "See you in the morning," he whispered and was gone.

By morning the *Fitz*'s gear was southwest of them due to the higher drift speed of the warmer water. Having eased into cooler water, their line had bunched up, giving the sharks a lot of slack with which to play. And play they did. Tommy spent the morning commiserating with the skipper of the *Fitz* assuring him conditions had really gone to hell overnight and that it was surely time to move along. The crew of the *Cap'n Fitz* started working on piles of shark snarls about the time the *Tecumseh* gang waded into a deck-load of 125 swordfish. The skipper of the *Fitz* had more time to talk that afternoon. Determined not to be caught twice, Tommy steamed *Tecumseh* north on autopilot while they cleaned fish, and only lay-to once shrouded by fog inside the lobster gear. As the afternoon wore on, *Tecumseh* kept hearing updates on the slow progress of repairs to the *Fitz*'s gear and the apparent lethargy that had come over the crew, who were acting like they had a trip of fish instead of a skunk. Finally the hapless skipper announced that he thought they would take a night off to look for a less sharky piece of water while unsnarling the rest of their gear. Tommy masked his delight on hearing this decision. He wished the *Fitz*'s skipper happy hunting, promising to get in touch when he got re-situated on fish.

Over the next five days, *Tecumseh*'s take of swordfish slowly dropped off as the bluedog catch increased. By their tenth set the weather had deteriorated. With the wind piping up to 30 knots from the southwest, Tommy needed full throttle to keep the lunging vessel on the gear. On deck, Fran and Lenny were trying to keep up with wrestling hooks and branchlines away from the sharks. Sammy was hauling and coiling the unsharked branchlines and Tommy was hauling and coiling floats in one pilothouse door and chucking them out the other into the ball pile. These emergency measures came to a temporary halt when Lenny handed the overextended captain a shark line instead of a float. Tommy grabbed his ripper, gave the branchline a mighty heave and leaned over the rail to dispatch another bluedog. At that moment *Tecumseh* rolled down and Tommy came face to face with an 200-pound mako shark. Recoiling from the near collision, he reared back only to hit his head on the railing behind him. As *Tecumseh* fell off the gear, Lenny finally noticed the bedraggled figure crouched against the pilothouse ladder doggedly hanging on to the mako branchline. Helping Tommy back into the pilothouse, Lenny dismissed the incident. "It's a young man's racket,

Cap." He closed the door as he left and returned to help Sam and Franny hoist the mako aboard.

By the middle of the last section Tommy had regained his composure and just then caught a glimpse through the port hole in the port pilothouse door of a vessel close aboard. The motion of the two vessels allowed only fleeting opportunities to view each other but Tommy immediately recognized the green hulled double-ender as the *Sandra Ann* from Portland.

"*Tecumseh*, *Sandra Ann*, talk to me on channel six, Tommy, if you can let go of the wheel long enough to switch channels." The deep, reassuring voice of Mainer Bill Bradshaw had a comforting effect on Tommy. He switched channels and clutched the mike in one hand as he steered with the other.

"So what brings you out in such nastiness, I see you're not dumb enough to be hauling gear in this garbage."

"We've been pickin' some good fish out of a layer of squid to the east a bit but a Jap factory trawler started towing through the gear and we weren't going to find all the pieces if we kept at it in this slop. You been listening to the weather?"

"No, what are they giving?"

"No good. There's a tropical depression made up on the Blake Plateau that's puckering up at Hatteras. Sounds like something we might want to get west of."

"Mercy, well, we needed a rest. These kids are working me to death. How fast is she coming?"

"T'was twelve while she was in warm water but forecast to pick up forward speed when she leaves the Stream. No sign of recurving to the east yet."

That's not nice at all," Tommy concluded. "I'm outta here when the end buoy comes aboard."

"Good idea, talk to you tonight after the 6:20."

The Tempest

Tommy wasted no time heading *Tecumseh* west-northwest on autopilot at the end of the haul. While the crew on deck stowed every piece of movable fishing gear in the whaleback, he removed radar reflectors from the hyflyer poles and replaced turbine ventilators to the galley with clamshell covers that could be clamped shut. With preparations completed, the crew went forward. As Tommy waited for the 6:20 weather, he hunched over his NOAA chart 13003 that covered the east coast from Hatteras to Nova Scotia. Walking off the mileage with his dividers he determined the disturbance had to cover 420 miles to intercept him and he had to cover 180 miles to escape. If the storm averaged 20 knots, *Tecumseh* had to do eight or better to avoid a near miss. If he didn't have 450 fish aboard he probably would have been steaming south toward Bermuda to get behind the storm. He weighed the risk he was taking. He had lost his seam to the sharks so he had to move anyway. Given the probability that the storm would eventually turn east he finally decided it was a better bet to go west even though he would be sacrificing some sea-room choices.

The 6:20 weather was all about hurricane Dora with a forward speed of 16 knots, forecast to increase in size and intensity. The weather service was being cagey about the landfall so preparations "should not be postponed."

Bill Bradshaw's voice had none of the urgency of the weather service broadcaster. "What do you make of them apples, Tommy?"

"Sounds like your everyday, run-of-the-mill hurricane."

"Well it looks to be slacking off here a tad, maybe we'll get 12 hours of steaming weather and a chance to change fuel filters before the good stuff arrives."

"I'm going to lean on it a bit, Bill. Sure would be nice to get on the lee side of Mama."

"That it would," replied Bradshaw. "Guess we'll see you in P'town if things get hairy in the bay."

"Yah, well, keep me posted. Talk to you after the 12:20."

Fran brought the smell of broiled steak with her through the lee pilothouse door. "Your ribeye's ready to go. What am I eatin', *Sandra Ann*'s dust?"

"Yah," replied Tommy. "He has to get a healthy ten out of her to make Portland in time if nothing changes. We're steering 310 degrees for now."

"Three ten it is; nice to have a weather man out front lettin' us know what to expect."

"Right now I wouldn't mind tradin' places with him," Tommy said as he went out the door.

Fran's Story

Franny held the wheel gently. The southwester was slacking off and there was less white water but every so often the starboard rail would bury and hesitate before rolling back. As the surface chop diminished, a long, low, barely perceptible swell from the southwest replaced it. Franny knew it for what it was. Raised on North Carolina's outer banks, she grew up on hurricanes. Many a time she had helped her parents load their belongings into fish boxes until their tarp-covered pickup truck sagged out the driveway, dragging her father's fishing skiff behind, headed for higher ground across the causeway to Columbia on the mainland. It was after one such exodus when they returned once again to a house full of sand, that her mother had taken her brother and gotten on the next ferry out of Ocracoke to start a new life in New Bern. Franny was too busy to miss her mother. Joining her father on the water was all she ever wanted. They seined rockfish, gill-netted mullet and mackerel and trapped eels, whelk and crabs. She missed a lot of school but her father insisted she bring her books home and they would study together at the kitchen table after the dinner dishes were put away. On the rare occasions that her mother's name was mentioned, her father would get a wistful, faraway look in his eyes and say, "Anyone can make a living out here in the summer." Franny understood her father because he explained everything in fishing terms. She'd never forget the argument she had overheard her parents having over whether to limit her extracurricular activities. Her father had stuck up for her saying, "If you crowd the girl now she'll mor'n likely go ape when she gets offshore and has a little sea-room." His most complimentary assessment of another human was to say they "could really haul some gear." She spent ten marvelous years fishing with him before he "passed over the bar."

They had set a hundred fathoms of ratty old 6-inch mesh across the channel a mile south of the bridge to Manteo. It was slack low water, a little before dawn and a little before the season. They were just going to check it out to see if there were any serious rockfish about. Drifting at the end of the set, they drank coffee from a thermos. The senior Miller had a smoke while Franny watched the lights of the odd car going to and fro on the bridge. About the time Franny noticed the tag line to the net was getting taut, there was a splash in the distance. She shined her headlamp toward the net. All the floats had disappeared. All she could see was roiling water and boils of sand and mud.

"Holy horse feathers," whispered Miller. "We better get this thing aboard!" He hauled and she picked 100 pounds every 10 fathom of net. They were half way to the end buoy when Franny looked up to see them drifting right toward the bridge with the flooding tide. The light of day promised to expose their clandestine caper at any moment.

"Time to rope her in, Dad," wailed Franny as she took up a position opposite him and started to haul the net, fish and all, into one big pile. Miller smiled at her.

"Bout time for ol' Lester to cross the bridge in his little green truck on his way to work, ain't it?" He asked. Franny grinned. Miller's laugh sounded like a panting dog.

"We'd be cotton pickin' fish in a barrel wouldn't we?" Franny started to laugh.

"After all the times he's been a day late and a dollar short chasing us, like as not he'll empty that shiny 44 right into our engine block." Franny was having trouble breathing between hauling and laughing.

"Jeeze! Dad, would you please shut up and haul," she pleaded.

"One thing's for sure," he continued with watery eyes, "the bugger'll want us alive so's he can lecture us while he carries us back and forth between jail and the courthouse."

Franny's stomach hurt as much as her back by the time they topped the stack of net and fish with the end buoy. She looked up to see a small traffic jam developing on the bridge above them. She gave the outboard lanyard a pull. Her prayers were drowned out by a roar from the old Seahorse Johnson. As they planed away down the channel, she silently thanked her old man for all the times he had insisted she change the fuel filters one more time. Her father lay down on the pile of net. He linked the fingers of his hands on his chest, closed his eyes and a broad smile came across his face. He was still smiling as they pulled up to the boat-ramp but his color was as gray as shark skin.

Franny was shattered. She went through the motions for awhile but quickly realized she was a team fisher. She wasn't on the water to escape as were so many of her father's friends. When the skipper of the longliner *Tecumseh* hailed her in Wanchese to buy her catch of Spanish mackerel for bait, he also inquired if she knew anyone who might replace a departed crew member. She followed the mackerel aboard and liked what she saw. After cooking the evening meal, she was hired.

The Gathering Storm

Lenny and Sam stood two-hour watches after Fran. This put Tommy back on watch for the 12:20 weather. Now the weather bureau was giving Long Island and its dense population a lot of attention as the first place the storm could get to on its present course. Tommy plotted the coordinates of the center and could see a slight easterly turn that the weather bureau had ignored. It could have been a random wobble but the forward speed now at 18 knots made this unlikely. Hurricanes usually accelerated when they start to recurve to the east. Tommy keyed his mike as he walked off the storm's new course and speed with his dividers.

"*Sandra Ann*, *Tecumseh*, you still up, Bill?"

"Yo, Tommy. Whataya make ah them apples?"

"Right now it looks like you'll make it inside and we'll end up outside."

"Yeah, Tommy, and if it goes west of us I don't know if I want to be inside. P'town is no picnic in a southerly."

"Least you'll have plenty of room. They'll all be in Sandwich basin or Pamet River."

"I might wait for you. If it goes west we can hang up at Peaked Hills, if it goes east we'll get a free ride around Race Point."

"I sure as hell don't like being that close and not be buttoned up. You might find a good anchorage behind Wood End if you don't mind getting covered with sand," Tommy finally suggested.

"Yeah, good anchorage if it doesn't go east."

"O.K. I give up, talk to you after the 6:20."

"Sleep well, Tommy."

It was calm when Tommy got off watch. A few of the brighter stars could be seen through a haze that gave each one of them a halo. There was a smell of copper in the air. He went forward to the galley, poured himself a cup of milk and sat at the galley table eating chocolate chip cookies Fran had left out. Looking at the soundly sleeping figures of Sam and Fran gave him a jolt of anxiety. Apparently he was the only one aboard with anything to worry about. He had a momentary urge to shake them awake and tell them at least to put on life jackets if they weren't going to worry with him. He finally concluded he should take their serenity as a compliment, washed out his cup and went aft to sleep until the 6:20 weather.

A murky gray morning dawned grudgingly. Only an increasing swell differentiated the sea from the saturated atmosphere. The weather bureau had moved the landfall of the hurricane east from Long Island to Block Island. The forward speed was up to 22 knots with winds in the dangerous east semicircle over one hundred knots. Bill Bradshaw got back to Tommy after the 6:20. "Think I've got time to run fair wind to Gloucester, Tommy. Then I won't have to buck the nor'wester to get to Portland tomorrow."

"Sounds like a plan," answered Tommy. "Looks like we'll be lucky to make P'town if she speeds up anymore. Talk to you at one o'clock," he promised as Franny entered the pilothouse.

"You've got a stack of French toast down there," she announced. "We still headed three ten degrees?"

"You got it. And don't waste any time, we're threadin' a needle at the other end."

"I'm not about to miss last call on account of any piss ass hurricane!" Franny declared.

Down forward, Lenny was replacing a stack of French toast that had disappeared when Sammy woke up unexpectedly. "Smelled

French toast, figgered Franny was plannin' to go shopping, thought I'd get up and give you guys a hand," Sam explained between mouthfuls. Tommy poured a cup of coffee and took a plate of toast, fresh off the griddle, from Lenny.

"Well, we've got last call and shopping on the activities list. Lenny, what are your plans for P'town?" asked Tommy, giving Len a chance to make light of their situation.

"Getting past Peaked Hill shoals will really make my day, Captain," Hill muttered.

"Ah-ha," Tommy slathered each layer of his stack of toast with butter. He found Lenny's anxiety comforting. "First things first from a man with experience in the field of saving lives and protecting property at sea." He filled the trough in the top of his pile of toast with maple syrup and glanced at Len, who had turned dead serious. Tommy kicked himself for talking business at a mealtime. He waved his fork above his French toast and softly sang:

"If you want to get to heaven, let me tell you what to do.
Just grease yourself with a mutton stew.
Along come the Devil with the outstretched hand
And you slip right through to the Promised Land."

No less an authority than the *United States Coast Pilot* refers to Cape Cod as "a long peninsula jutting eastward from the mainland of Massachusetts like an arm bent upward at the elbow." For those who would hope to navigate her waters successfully a more appropriate analogy might be the curled up tail of a scorpion or stingray. Better yet, the tassel between the eyes of the goosefish, promising the unsuspecting a snack only to provide its owner with a meal. Provincetown harbor is called "one of the best harbors on the Atlantic coast" with "excellent holding ground," but to get there one must pass the bones of hundreds of once able seagoing vessels.

Tommy finished his breakfast and poured himself a traveler. "Before you guys hit the sack again, how about helping Fran furl the riding sail." Stirring in some sugar and cream he added, "You might want to double up on the gaskets."

All morning they plowed across an ever-increasing swell toward the ever-darkening western sky. The weather bureau forecasts became more frequent but always seemed to lag behind real time. By ten o'clock, the storm's landfall had again been moved east, this time to Cuttyhunk Island. Tommy heaved a sigh of relief. He'd made it to the "navigable semicircle" west of the storm's center. The 12:20 didn't shed any new light on their situation, but Bill Bradshaw filled Tommy in at one o'clock. "We're picking up Don Kent on the tube, Tommy. They're clocking 80 knots easterly at Block Island. He's got it slicing up Muskeget channel coming out Pollack Rip. You've got it made."

"What have you got there, Bill?"

"Forty, 45 knots easterly at Eastern point. How many hours 'til you're inside?"

"Three and a half, four. Depends on what the tide decides to do."

"Well, we'll be standing by with the updates as soon as we find something solid to tie up to, Tommy, all the best."

Skating the Faces

Tommy looked out the port pilothouse door as he hung up the mike to see the sea surface to the south turning black with white trim. Sammy was at the starboard door. "We going to skate the faces, Cap?"

"Looks like it, Sam. How about getting Franny to make up a few sandwiches and a jug of Joe while she can still cut the bologna."

Sammy nodded and went forward. Tommy listened to the calling and distress frequency. The Corps of Engineers had just closed the doors in the hurricane dike at New Bedford. Immediately there was a chorus of complaints from fishing boats in Buzzards Bay that had started for home an hour too late. The Corps never answered these laments but it seemed that every boat that had made it to safety behind the dike was eager to tell the stragglers what a bunch of greedy bastards they were. Threats and insults in several languages filled the air. Tommy was smiling when Sammy got back with their box lunch. "What's for dinner, Sam?"

"B.L.T.s and ham and cheese. You hungry?"

"We work it right and we can make four meals out of it today."

"I can't stand the smell of bacon," Sammy complained as he rooted around in the plastic bag. "I found it helps if you eat it," he said as he handed Tommy a sandwich.

The first rain squall rattled on the after windows of the pilot-house as they finished their sandwiches. "You want to take it for a while, Sam? We're going to hold 310 until we get in 100 feet of water. Then we'll just hold that depth right around the corner into the harbor. I'll try to cross check with radar and Loran, but we can't rely on 'em when all hell breaks loose."

"Just like the good old days," Sammy observed as he took the wheel. "What's Fran say? 'Anyone can make a livin' out here in the summer.'"

"Yah, we're steaming into a hurricane and she's down there with a bag of dirty laundry, makin' out the grocery list."

They were silent as the wind began to rise. It sang through the antenna farm atop the pilothouse. It turned the backs of the swells that passed under *Tecumseh* into white washboards. At first they could distinguish rain squalls from the spray torn from the wave tops, and for a while the rain dampened the effects of the wind on the sea surface. Soon, however, these components blended, traveling horizontally across the sea surface, past *Tecumseh*, giving the occupants of the pilothouse the feeling of sitting backwards on a high-speed train. This wind-driven water objected to every obstacle in its path. What had started as a rattle on the back of the pilothouse, became a constant ripping sound that diminished only for brief moments when a large wave gave the vessel momentary shelter.

Steering a boat in a following sea is a ticklish business. If a vessel is big enough and tough enough, one can simply run the engines slow astern into the gale and hope all the hatches hold. Smaller vessels must employ finesse to avoid broaching. This is complicated by the difference in the effectiveness of the rudder from the moment the vessel is wallowing in the trough to the moment she accelerates down the face of a wave. Whatever rudder angle is used to keep the boat lined up in the trough must be reduced with the increase in speed that she develops on the face of the wave. At night, the direction of the flow of vapor passing over the pilothouse can help the helmsman keep the vessel lined up. When visibility is zero, the helmsman resorts to the basic rule of bike riding: steer in the direction of the list. A compass or autopilot is useless in a rough sea because its dampened reactions are too slow to answer the immediate needs of the vessel. A vessel maneuvering to survive needs unlimited sea room. To seek shelter often means exposing it to some of the worst conditions.

Sammy loved skating the faces of waves in a following sea. He had the waves classified. There were "twisters" with uneven tops that heeled the boat as if she was going around a corner backwards. There were "humpers," white swells that had recently broken. There were "combers" that broke just behind the boat wrapping white arms of foam around the pilothouse. These roaring walls of phosphorus turned red and green under the running lights at night and filled the waist of the *Tecumseh* rail to rail.

And then there were "butt-bangers." Butt-bangers announced themselves with a thud as they broke over the stern of the vessel, throwing a halo of green water over the pilothouse. The extra energy of a butt-banger provided acceleration that resulted in a longer skate in the hands of an expert. Sammy loved butt-bangers. Tommy didn't love butt-bangers. Eventually one was going to fill up the lifeboat and drive it through the back of the pilothouse. Out of respect for the captain's feelings, Sammy never called butt-bangers by name. He would simply nod and smile after a good B.B. Tommy would nod and grimace.

Halfway to the Cape, Dora tried to get personal. Every time Sammy steered into a black hole, tons of ocean would follow. He couldn't see where he was going until the next wave lifted them out of the foam and sent them barreling down the next wave. It was all Sammy could do to keep *Tecumseh* on her feet. Tommy stayed wedged in the pilot seat with his foot against the bulkhead. His thoughts were of the accounts of schooners that having crossed the banks in a blow at night, awoke in the morning to find sand on deck. As it was they picked up four knots in the following seas and made Race Point in two hours, just as the wind slammed around from the northwest. After a wild fair-wind ride to Wood End in whiteout all the way, they turned north into the harbor and for the first time fought the storm head-on struggling to the dock into the teeth of the gale. Wind-driven spray, sand and leaves plastered the pilothouse windows. But the rain had stopped and the tension in the pilothouse drained away as the dim light from the opened doghouse doors silhouetted two figures in foul weather gear moving aft to get down the mooring lines.

"I think it's laying down." Sam uttered the time-honored observation reserved for such occasions.

"Yeah," answered Tommy, "the stop signs are laying down, the street lights are laying down, the telephone poles are laying down."

Provincetown

They tied up next to a ladder in the lee of the fishhouse where *Tecumseh* rode the wraparound swells like a horse on a merry-go-round. Lenny helped Sam get his dad's opah out of the fish hold and up the ladder to the dock. Then Sammy was gone, dragging the fish on a box hook with one hand, carrying a bread bag in the other. Lenny joined Fran and Tommy, who were sitting at the galley table with their hands wrapped around steaming cups of tea-colored liquid. Lenny thought they might be in the middle of some seance of thanksgiving until he sniffed at a third cup on the table and winced.

"Sugarcane brandy, lad," growled Tommy. "Settle your stomach, calm your nerves."

Lenny took a swallow. The brew had a life of its own. He felt it warm his heart, then his lungs and finally spread out in his stomach like the roots of a tree. He sat down, hugging the warm cup, closed his eyes and took another swallow. It occurred to him that this was the very spot from which the bishop dispensed holy water during the blessing of the fleet. He considered it blessing enough just to be here. He took a third swallow and was sure he could hear strains of "Eternal Father, strong to save" as the backlash of the storm eddied around the fish house, worrying *Tecumseh*'s rigging like a determined terrier snorting down the hole of some escaped rodent. "Whose arm hath bound the restless wave," thought Lenny.

They finished their drinks slowly with little talk until Franny turned to Len and asked, "Before you get too comfortable, would you mind running a bag of clothes up to the laundromat so it will be ready tomorrow?"

"Sure," responded Lenny as he washed out his cup. "I'm too comfortable now."

He grabbed the laundry and his jacket from the doghouse and started up the fish house ladder. As he reached the top something warm and wet smacked him in the kisser. Between licks he was relieved to feel the whiskers of a very large dog. "Get 'um Coke!" he heard a female voice encouraging the mugger. "Must be some tasty cup cake by now."

"I give up," gagged Lenny. "Call off your mutt!"

"Now, now, dune hopper; you're in no position to insult the canine." Lenny recognized Angela's voice.

"Please control your companion, ma'am, before he knocks me off the frigging ladder."

"Ooops, wash his mouth out, Coke, wash his mouth out good now." Coke did his best to follow Angie's instructions until Lenny finally hoisted the laundry bag up over the cap log and could use two hands to climb onto the dock.

"Where the hell have you guys been?' Angie demanded. She sounded like she might have walked all the way from Dennis looking for them.

"We been skatin' the faces with Sammy," said Lenny. "He's headed to his dad's."

"Ta hell he is!" spat Angie. "I just came from there. We've been listening to the radio for six hours trying to get a line on you assholes."

"Guess we were busy."

"Busy! I'll show you busy. Where you going with that bag? We're not quitting because of a little weather are we?"

"It's laundry," he bristled, "Fran wants to get it to the laundromat so it will be ready tomorrow."

"Come on, the power's been on and off all evening but she might still be there." Leaning into the wind, they walked up the dock. The town looked like it might have before the electric lines finally made it from the mainland. Kerosene lanterns gleamed through kitchen windows, revealing people gathered around eating, drinking, reading. At the laundry a short jolly lady was folding clothes by candlelight.

"We're through for today but I'll have it by nine o'clock if they have power back on in the morning." Lenny thanked her and they went back out into the night.

"Come on, let's see if he stopped by the *Northern Edge* on the way home." She and Coke struck out down the street without waiting for a reply.

The hostile weather and lack of electric power seemed to have piqued rather than diminished the party mood at the *Northern Edge*. The clientele was doing its best to compensate for the silent TV, and the band played bravely on over its dead electronic aids. No doubt the spirit of camaraderie had something to do with the amount of alcohol the barkeep was putting in a tall drink he had dubbed "The Tempest." The scene Angie and Lenny walked in on was every bit as wild as the one they left outside. They ordered two Tempests and observed from a safe distance the sensual writhing on the small dance floor. Candles and lanterns illuminated the smoke-choked room in subtle shades of neon, making the patrons who were already feeling brotherly, look brotherly.

Lenny cruised for a bit while Angie interrogated a couple of wallflowers. He had picked up two more Tempests on his return. Giving Angie her drink, he whispered in her ear, "I can't tell the difference between the guys and the dolls."

Angie whispered back, "The girl's pants go up the crack of their asses." Sipping his Tempest, Lenny studied the crowd over the rim of his glass, pondering eternal mysteries. His manner agitated Angie. She took his glass from him and dragged him toward the rhythmic melee'. Lenny was feeling pretty relaxed and could have enjoyed himself if Angie hadn't fixed him with an intimidating stare. Lenny simply closed his eyes and let the music flow over his body like the sugarcane brandy had done internally. Floating in the half-light, surrounded by pandemonium, he did a hybrid limbo-sun dance that seemed to provoke some oooos and aaaahs. He had totally relaxed when he felt something warm and soft brush his cheek. Without interrupting his generous flow, he cracked one eye to locate Angie. She was behind him, holding her powder blue sweater, a sleeve cuff in each hand, massaging her back as if drying off after a shower. Lenny cracked the other eye to see flashing blue light reflecting on the ceiling over the windows at the front of the bar and the bulky figure of a man headed their way through the crowd from the same direction. Lenny collected himself, got his arms around Angie and to the obvious disappointment of the gathering, hustled her toward the swinging doors leading to the kitchen. Angie had her sweater on by the time they reached the loading platform where Coke was entertaining the femur of a large beef critter. From there Angie took the lead, "Come on, we'll get our coats tomorrow." She led them up a side street toward the flashing red light atop the Pilgrim's monument. The streetlights came on as they climbed the leaf-strewn sidewalk up Monument Hill. The trees at the top had lost all their foliage and joined the power lines to make a moan that covered several octaves. Just shy of the top of the hill, Angie led Lenny up the steps of a bed and breakfast studio overlooking the harbor. They stared out a picture window in the dark, looking across the bay at the beam of light from Highland that winked in their direction every five seconds. Lenny marveled at how the same light that shouted "danger, look out" to the mariner became a benign curiosity once one was ashore.

"I'm going to shower," Angie announced, as she turned on a bedside lamp and disappeared into the bathroom. Lenny turned on the TV to a news program, kicked off his shoes and laid down on the bed to watch storm damage reports. He had dozed off by the time Angie returned in a white terry cloth robe, her hair wrapped in a towel atop her head.

"It's all yours," she smiled. "Let me know if you want Coke to scrub your back."

Lenny showered. He was so exhausted he imagined at times that his body might, at any moment, go down the drain with the soap suds. He soaked until the water began to get cool. Drying himself, he wrapped in the two remaining towels and returned to the studio. Angie was curled up on the far side of the bed with her back to him. The muted TV showed a weatherman projecting the path of a hurricane passing between Halifax and Sable Island. Lenny gently lowered himself to the bed. For a moment Angie didn't move. Then she rolled toward him and put her head on his shoulder. The towel came off her head. Her hair poured over his chest.

"Did you do any good?" she murmured in her sleep.

During the night, the chatter of a helicopter awoke Lenny. Without moving, he watched the flashing lights of the aircraft work upwind past the picture window. Somewhere close to the monument, the 'copter feathered her blades for a moment, then put the pitch back on and lifted off to be lost in the whisper of the wind in the eaves.

Lenny awoke from a deep sleep to a painfully bright day. Angie and Coke were gone. He slipped into his clothes, which included the damp underwear he had washed the night before, and headed downtown. Coke, using his bone for a pillow, lay asleep in the sun outside the laundromat. Angie was inside folding a pile of clothes, tears streaming down her face. Lenny caught the eye of the jolly lady of the night before. She shook her head. Lenny folded laundry with shaking hands. When all the clothes were in the bag, Angie gave Lenny his jacket and a hug, wiping her tears on his shirt.

"I've got to go tell the old man," she murmured and was out the door.

Small pods of people fell silent as Lenny passed on his way to the boat. Tommy and Fran were drinking coffee in the pilothouse. Apparently Sammy had gotten into a friendly argument with a biker about the intensity of the gale. To settle the disagreement they had climbed on the biker's machine and gone tearing down Route 6 to clock the wind speed. Before they satisfied their curiosity they ran into a sand drift that had been blown across the road. The biker had broken a collar bone. Sammy had been airlifted to Brighton Marine Hospital in a Coast Guard helicopter.

"We're going to take out fish in an hour," Tommy said. "Why don't you get something to eat."

Lenny went forward. He poured a cup of orange juice and sat at the galley table staring at Sammy's empty bunk. His mind raced, reshuffling the facts he had been told to somehow reach an acceptable explanation. Every time he took a sip of orange juice, reality returned to perch on the edge of Sammy's bunk. He washed out his cup and went on deck.

The fishhouse lent them a man to guide the strapped fish out of the fish hold. His wisps of white hair were kept in check by a faded blue engineer's cap. He had thin lips and squinty eyes that were the color of the sky at dawn. He wore yellow slickers and when he brought the weigh-out tally down to the pilothouse after they had finished unloading, he and Tommy started talking groundfish trawling. Tommy needed someone to take Sammy's place and it wasn't long before he sent John Buell up the street with Fran to get the rest of his gear and enough groceries to finish out the trip.

Off to the Northeast Channel

They left the dock an hour before sunset as the local fleet straggled back into the harbor from more sheltered moorings across the bay. The storm had left the town with the clean scrubbed look of winter. The waterfront was void of small craft. Anything that could have been moved had been taken in or blown away. Late afternoon sun reflected off the cluster of white homes framed by a light blue northern sky that seemed apologetic in its stillness. The crew of the *Tecumseh* went about their tasks in a zombie-like trance. Minor wrinkles and inconsistencies were met with unusual displays of aggravation. John Buell followed them about trying to be helpful without seeming patronizing. They left Sammy's bunk empty and gave Buell the top bunk opposite Lenny. Tommy saved mealtimes from being unbearably morose by silently rescinding the prohibition of fish-talk. John Buell did monologues on his best halibut trip to Georges Bank, his best haddock trip to Cashe's Ledge and best codfish trip to Parker's Ridge. During the 24 hours they steamed east, the crew of *Tecumseh* began to eat. Not a lot at first but slowly they were coaxed into going through the motions. Slowly they began to think fishing instead of what might be happening to Sammy.

Though the weather was perfect, they didn't look for swordfish that next day. At three in the afternoon they took up ten boxes of bait. At five, they passed some Canadian halibut trawl on the northeast peak of Georges. Tommy passed close by the hyflyer to check the current. It was drifting southeast. He idled *Tecumseh* northeast, watching as the sounder slowly etched the bottom from 50 down to 100 fathoms. Franny came aft with the smell of boiled corned beef and cabbage. "You need a wheel watch or are we going to lay to for dinner?" she asked staring off into a rosy sunset.

"We're where we want to be," Tommy answered with his head in the radar hood. Franny was silent for a moment then inquired calmly, "You want to harpoon that swordfish?"

Tommy's eyes followed hers. "You take the wheel," he whispered. "I'll call the gang on my way forward."

Franny never touched the throttle. She fell into the wake of the large black tail that left lazy S's in the surface and hardly moved the wheel until Tommy's right arm drove the harpoon out of sight. The warp tub emptied quickly but not before Tommy bent on another length of line to keep the fish from pulling the dart with the resistance of the 40-inch float in water deeper than they usually fished. Lenny got down a hyflyer that they put on the float line so they could find it in the dark after they ate. For the first time since leaving Provincetown there was hope around the dinner table.

After dinner they set up the deck as Tommy steamed up on the hyflyer that was being towed southeast by the harpooned swordfish. Clipping the end of the mainline to the harpoon float, Tommy brought *Tecumseh* around to the northeast and they started to set gear across the channel towards Brown's Bank. Two hours later as the water began to shoal approaching Brown's, they dropped the last bait and lighted hyflyer in the water. The night was pitch black, the weather dead calm. They never had to steam up to the end buoy until after breakfast the next morning. John Buell called it "Gentleman fishing." He took Lenny's float-coiling duties as Lenny moved up to coiling branchlines and Fran hauled and unclipped.

They hauled the first four sections in 65-degree water and never saw a fish. As they approached the middle of the channel, the surface temperature went up to 68 degrees and they had a dozen harpoon-sized fish before the water started to cool again. They went fishless for the last four sections, with the exception of the harpooned fish on the end buoy. The surface current moving southeast was being forced into the 150-fathom channel between Brown's and Georges Banks creating a five-mile-wide ribbon of warm water down the center of the channel. While they cleaned and iced the day's catch, Tommy pondered how to set the gear to take full advantage of this ribbon of warm water. They were wasting the gear in cold water at each end of the set. It was only acting as anchors to keep the hooks in the middle fishing the warm shallow water. If he got greedy and set straight down the middle of the ribbon, the hooks would sink through the warm layer and they could miss the fish completely. Before John Buell went below Tommy had him make up four two-legged bridles with clips at each end and one in the middle.

The Cat's Cradle

That night they clipped the legs of a bridle to the handles of one of the wash tubs used to stow branchlines and clipped the middle snap to the mainline under the end buoy. Starting in 65-degree water, Tommy steamed northeast, putting sections two through five in 68-degree water. Turning east, he put another tub in the middle of section six, after which he turned south and southwest, running back across the warm ribbon with sections seven through ten. Repeating the process, they put a tub in the middle of the eleventh section and crossed the ribbon a third time with sections twelve through fifteen. The last tub went on the end of the sixteenth section. By the end of the evening a pool had been organized on deck awarding $50 to the one who came closest to guessing the number of hours it was going to take to unsnarl Tommy's creation. One by one they came to the pilothouse to gaze at the radar image of what John Buell called the "captain's cat's cradle."

"No swordfish leaving the Gulf of Maine tonight!" Tommy pronounced in his own defense.

They didn't triple their catch the second night but 26 big fish put a list on *Tecumseh* until they were dressed and went below. After four nights they had 73 fish and the cat's cradle had successfully fished in a brisk southwester. There was a cold front coming but Tommy couldn't resist fishing for one more day. The migration would not last 'til they returned. The southwester diminished at sunset but at two in the morning the northwester arrived and they had to steam constantly to stay with the end buoy. Dawn revealed an angry-looking sea that would have been beautiful had they not been required to work in it.

Tommy waited for full light before picking up the end buoy. They hauled the first section and got back the second hyflyer before the mainline was parted off. They had no fish and Tommy could find nothing resembling a target on radar. Sea conditions created clutter on the radar out to two miles and when the hyflyers were standing up straight they were visible for only four miles. So Tommy started searching back and forth across the channel with the radar while the crew manned the masthead two at a time looking for orange polyballs. Each crossing took them two hours. After a crossing Tommy would steam southeast for an hour before re-crossing the channel again. After ten hours the sun was getting low, they were on the 500-fathom curve and had yet to see any sign of their gear. The only encouraging sign was the diminishing northwest wind.

Tommy idled the engine and called John and Lenny down from the masthead. He took one last long look at the radar and turned it off. Turning to the chart table he plotted their Loran position and pondered the evaporation of seventeen miles of gear. Finally he gave up searching for a logical answer and watched the sea lick at the lower limb of the settling sun. He was waiting for the green flash like one of the idle, rich and famous when a deep, inquisitive voice came over the VHF.

"*Tecumseh*, how long you plannin' to soak this gear?"

Tommy grabbed the mike, "Captain Bill," he declared. "You tell me where you are and I'll tell you how long it will take us to get there."

"We're out in about 1,000 fathoms. Your gear took quite a ride. So where are you now?"

"I don't know why you couldn't have told me that this morning. I could be on my way home by now," Tommy scolded.

“We were looking for our own gear this morning. You headed home?”

Tommy filled in Bradshaw on their five nights of successful fishing and Bill gave Tommy the loran numbers of his lost gear. Later that night they would trade places.

The following morning dawned crystal clear with a gentle northerly breeze. Tommy’s cat’s cradle had turned clockwise 90 degrees so they hauled north and south from east to west. They caught seven more big fish but the rest of the catch was composed of half a dozen juvenile swordfish, four 3-foot mackerel sharks and three smooth brown-skinned oil fish.

The Hard Way Home

Tommy was glad to turn *Tecumseh* toward home. He let the crew clean the last day's catch. Talking to Bradshaw, he relished the rare opportunity of putting the *Sandra Ann* on fish. The trip home is usually full of hope, with a feeling of relaxation among the salts and channel fever among the youthful. On *Tecumseh*, the respite from concern for Sammy dissolved. It was a somber crew that ate breakfast as they entered Pollack Rip the next morning.

Pollack Rip Channel runs from the northeast, past the tip of Monomoy into Nantucket Sound. It is a beautiful place in fair weather, with green breakers of every hue boiling over countless sandbars on both sides of the channel. In hard weather it can be very nasty with continuous breakers across the channel. This nastiness is compounded by a unique quirk of hydrography: the fair tide into the sound at Pollack Rip is an ebb tide. So if you lose power and go aground, the flood that comes to float you free will come from the west shoving you back toward one of the many angry shoals patiently waiting offshore. So it was cause for more than usual concern that Tommy heard a sharp crack as they cleared the southwest end of the channel, followed by a rumble that shook the whole vessel. Franny was sitting on the head in the engine room reading her latest Mademoiselle as Tommy descended the ladder, using the handrails as his only support. He flew to the deck plate over the stuffing box and jerked it noisily aside.

"Shit!" He reached for an open-end wrench wedged in the corner of a nearby battery box. Rhythmically he tightened four nuts holding the packing gland collar. This slowly stemmed the flow of water past the layers of packing unsettled by the wobbling of the cracked propeller shaft.

Tommy paused on the wing of the pilothouse to check for any traffic that might be headed to the west. Just discernible in the path of the sun was a destroyer-like silhouette. Taking the binoculars John Buell offered him, Tommy studied the approaching vessel. Without taking the glasses away from his eyes he addressed Buell. "I believe we have a real live Coast Guard 95-footer headed this way and she's empty handed!" He whistled a few bars of the Coast Guard anthem and picked up the VHF mike.

"Calling the Coast Guard vessel westbound in Pollack Rip channel, this is the fishing vessel *Tecumseh*, Whiskey Hotel 6288, you picking me up Captain?"

"This is the cutter *Cape Horn*, 95322 back to the vessel calling."

"This is the *Tecumseh*, Captain, we're disabled a mile-and-a-half ahead of you with a broken propeller shaft. Any chance of bumming a tow to the west'ard?"

"*Tecumseh*, *Cape Horn*; give me your location, the length and description of your vessel, home port, number of people aboard and the nature of your distress."

Tommy had radioed the necessary information by the time the 95-footer pulled alongside, backed down toward them from their windward side and tossed a messenger line aboard. Lenny and John made the towline fast and wrapped a length of fire hose around it where it passed through the towing chock. Slowly the cutter took the slack out of the towline, turning all the time to shape a course for Cross Rip. Slowly, obediently, *Tecumseh* turned to follow her. Tommy Martin was starting to relax as his vessel eased up to cruising speed when there came another snap from the engine room and a loud rumble from the stern of the boat. Tommy snatched the mike from the VHF radio.

"*Cape Horn*, *Tecumseh*. We've got a loose prop chewing up the rudder here, could you slow to a creep while we get a line on her?"

"Roger on that *Tecumseh*. How long do you expect that'll take?"

"Five minutes with any luck."

"Roger, *Tecumseh*. Going to slow, slow ahead. Keep us advised of your progress."

Tommy rattled off instructions: Johnny Buell to open the landing gate; Franny to stream a longline float back in the wake to act as a life buoy; Lenny to get a mooring line down from the lifeboat. He went below to snug the packing gland one more time and returned on deck with a facemask and snorkel. He was checking their speed through the water when he felt a tug on the mask. Lenny was standing behind him stripped down to his T-shirt and jeans.

"It's a young man's racket Cap'n," he said as he took the mask from Tommy.

"Fine," Tommy responded. "Get the eye of the mooring line on the first blade you come to and come back up the mooring line if you have enough air. If you're running short of air, go for the surface and grab the polyball."

Lenny nodded and adjusted the strap on the mask. He spit on the facemask, rubbed the saliva around the glass and rinsed the mask over the side. They paid out the mooring line with Lenny hanging on the eye until he was over the rudder. He gave a "thumbs up" and dove out of sight. A moment later he burst to the surface and grabbed the polyball line and was pulled back to the gate. Franny had a bucket of hot fresh water and a towel waiting for him. They made the mooring line fast and called the cutter to have another go at it. This time there was nothing but the swishing of bubbles from *Cape Horn*'s wake along *Tecumseh*'s hull to mark their progress.

Lenny toweled off in front of the Shipmate, put on dry clothes and crawled into his bunk to warm up. He began to wonder what it would be like to be on the "other end" of a Coast Guard boarding that was routine at the termination of a tow job. They would pretty surely end up in New Bedford to be close to a yard if anything else let go below the waterline. He wondered if they still had old "Spud" the drug-sniffing yellow Lab at the State Pier.

The convulsion that grabbed Lenny's body slammed his head and knees against his bunk boards. He came out of his bunk backwards, blankets and all, did a 180 in midair and landed on the settee with his head in his hands.

"Oh shit!" he moaned.

Franny, who had been mopping up his water tracks, rushed to his side and grabbed his shoulder.

"Are you all right?" she asked.

"It's Sammy," he moaned.

"Yah, we're gonna find out about Sammy, what's your problem?"

Lenny moaned again. "Sammy's got a bale in the engine room."

"You're shitting me," Franny declared.

"Tell me you're shitting me," she demanded.

"Would I shit you about a thing like that?" he asked, finally looking at her.

"Oh no! You're not shitting me," Franny decided.

Lenny told her the grim details. How the bale had come aboard the previous trip and how Sammy had persuaded him, a little too well as it turned out, to forget it existed. Franny looked at him for a long time, slowly shaking her head.

"Well, we got to tell the old man," she said with conviction. "We got to get rid of it."

"Oh shit," Lenny moaned, putting his head back in his hands.

They all stood in the pilothouse as Lenny told his story. Tommy listened without comment. When Lenny was through Tommy simply looked away toward the stern of the Coast Guard cutter *Cape Horn* and up to the wing of the bridge where a tow watch stood facing aft in his hooded jacket with a pair of binoculars hanging around his neck.

"Is there anything else that can go wrong this trip?" he asked no one in particular. There was silence.

He would have loved to chew out somebody. He would have loved to pick up the mike and say, "Alright mothers, you got me this time, come and get it!" But there is a reason an outnumbered band of revolutionary fishermen held off the British at Throg's Neck. Working in an environment that will take your life if you give an inch teaches participants who love life to avoid that possibility. Tommy worked on a plan while letting Lenny sweat.

"O.K. Fran and John, turn on the deck water and start washing rugs. Lenny, go find the bale and bring it forward wrapped in a carpet and drop it down into the fish hold before you put the carpet on deck. Go back and get the rest of the carpets. Hop down into the hold with your little bundle of joy. Hand Franny up some chow or ice or soft drinks, whatever. Then split the bale in half and put each chunk in the bottom of a bait box. Cover it with mackerel and top each box with ice. Get back on deck as soon as you can and scrub rugs with John so Franny can go forward and make lunch. Be cool; no sudden moves. We don't want to wake the kid if he's dozing."

They left the pilothouse one at a time. The interior decks of *Tecumseh* were fitted with rubber-backed rugs to soak up water and prevent slipping. They needed scrubbing after every trip, a perfect distraction for undercover work. When rinsed, the rugs were hung out to drain and dry. With the scrubbing completed the skullduggery was set in motion. Lenny took the watch. The others went forward to fine tune their plan as they ate.

"Fran," Tommy started, "I'm hoping the boarding party isn't ready to jump aboard when we put the lines ashore. If they do, we're cooked. These guys have been on patrol, so it's likely they'll make for the main gate and let a gang from the base handle it. I want you to get cleaned up and bullshit any watch guard they put on the dock while they get a boarding party together. Tell him anything it takes to get him on the hook. Once you've got him there, tell him we've got some bait that has to get to the freezer before it closes and hold your breath."

Tommy paused and looked from Franny to John. "Any suggestions?"

Buell had a broad grin on his face. "Shit Cap; move over Arthur Miller!"

Franny wasn't smiling. "Miller and Miller," she drawled, "you're going to owe me bigtime."

They got tied to the dock, the watch showed up, Franny bullshitted him and Tommy watched with elevated pulse as his crew, lined up three abreast, started walking the two boxes of "bait" toward a gate to the street. Tommy ticked off the possible disasters that could befall a plan so close to completion when a large yellow forklift came rumbling up the dock behind the escapees. There was a short exchange during which Lenny looked back at Tommy. Tommy didn't move. "Be cool, move slowly," he prayed.

They started again down the dock holding the boxes balanced on the forks of the machine. All went smoothly for a few yards until some bumps in the pavement shook the forks violently and ice started slithering off the mackerel.

"Whoa, whoa!" pleaded Lenny, waving his arms.

"It's only ice," shouted the Coast Guardsman. "You're on the way to the freezer."

"Ice is good," moaned Lenny. "I love ice," he said beseechingly as he got between the forks and grabbed the handles of the fish boxes.

Franny looked at John stifling a giggle. "Ice *is* good," she agreed.

"Yeah," John chimed in with conviction. "We love ice."

He grabbed the box handle opposite Lenny and led the trio away from the forklift and its puzzled operator. John Buell's head was bowed, his eyes closed. Tears streamed down his cheeks.

Their route to the freezer crossed a four-lane street with an island in the middle. They got stranded on the island when the light turned green. Traffic roared by them on either side. As the light turned yellow, guttural snarls announced the arrival of three Harleys with six big, leathered-up individuals, half of whom hadn't shaved since Nam.

"Where yah to with them tinkers?" asked the biggest biker.

"Headed for the freezer," John pointed to the loading dock 50 yards away.

"Give you 20 bucks for the whole mess," the biker offered.

"I don't know," John replied with furrowed brow. "Do you think we can let them go for 20 bills?" he asked Lenny.

"If it's O.K. with Franny, it's O.K. with me," Lenny responded.

"It's been a long damn day," observed Franny. "I might just up and give you my share."

The bikers took possession of the bait as if choreographed. The rider on the middle bike was holding on to nothing but the two box handles as the lights changed and off they roared, three abreast, down the street like a circus act.

"Walk, don't run to the nearest bar," Franny instructed as she led them toward a nearby purple neon sign announcing the location of the *Universal Joint*. It was an hour and a half before Tommy joined them.

"The duty officer wants to meet you wetbacks before we leave for the yard," he said, "and Lenny m'boy, your buddy Spud did everything but pee in my boot trying to find that bale."

They had downed three rounds, their shared memories mellowing as they drank, when the silhouettes of two of the Harley boys filled the doorway. They spied Tommy, sauntered over, picked him up by the elbows and walked him out the door. When Tommy's crew caught up with them, the six bikers had him up against a brick wall. The largest was taking out of his pocket what looked like two 10-dollar stacks of quarters rolled up tight.

"Them tinkers was real garbage," the Hog driver growled, nose to nose with Tommy, "but the shit is out of this world!"

They all howled with laughter as he stuffed two rolls of bills into Tommy's shirt pocket, so enthusiastically the pocket ripped partly off. When the hilarity subsided the biker grabbed Tommy by the shoulders. "We were real sorry to hear about your harpooner," he murmured softly, "can we buy you a drink?"

The Yard

The shipyard tug bumped alongside as they were finishing breakfast the next morning. It was overcast with a light drizzle that didn't help to lift their spirits. As the towboat nudged *Tecumseh* across the harbor, Len and John set up the deck to take out the fish. The dealer's truck was waiting at the end of the shipyard wharf. Unloading went smoothly until they reached the biggest fish in the bottom of the hold. The portable scales on the back of the truck bottomed out when the hefty carcasses were lowered on them. The guy with the Fu Manchu wanted to cut the big fish in two to weigh them. Tommy groaned and Fran smiled shaking her head. They'd both seen weigh-out slips come back with the lower "chunk" price for fish weighed like this. Tommy sent John and Fran in her truck with the last of the catch to witness the weigh-out at the fishhouse. After turning *Tecumseh* over to the yard crew, Len and Tommy climbed into the skipper's truck and headed for High Head where Sammy's ashes would be spread later that day.

The Farewell

The drizzle was letting up by the time they reached Orleans. Looking at his watch, Tommy pulled off the rotary and eased into the parking lot of the Orleans Inn. They took a table overlooking the Town Cove, ordered rum punches and oyster stew. A large flock of geese was feeding in the eelgrass on a shoal not far from shore. The geese made Tommy happy. He never passed this way without missing the duck farm that had become a McMansion housing development overlooking his ocean. This place used to belong to the animals, birds, and fish. Now it was covered with imported golf course grass, granite sea walls, and palatial houses that were empty most of the year. He was jerked out of his moody reflections as Fran and John entered the dinning room quite pleased to have spotted a familiar truck from the rotary.

They left plenty of time to get to High Head but the parking lot was almost full when they arrived. A bunch of motorcycles had braved the wet weather. Lenny was no sooner out of the truck than a heavy black object hit the back of his legs. He collapsed to one knee and buried his face in Coke's burly neck as the grief that he had thus far denied overwhelmed him. The big dog licked Lenny's neck with slow comforting strokes. When he had regained his composure, Lenny looked up to meet the gaze of a man he immediately recognized as Sammy's father. He stood and hugged the man but had not gained enough self-control to speak. No matter. Santos Sr. hadn't bothered to speak English until his son's accident. He'd had no need too. Having had time to manage his own grief, he was in a position to help Sammy's crewmates with theirs.

They walked together until Mr. Cruz looking ahead, turned to Lenny.

"I think Angela is headed for the ocean, Son. You better go save her."

Glossary

Block—pulley.

Breeches buoy—beach to vessel rescue system used by early life saving services.

Broach—to be forced beam to following seas.

Cathead—revolving, smooth, bronze cylinder around which a line is wrapped giving a seaman the mechanical advantage to lift heavy weights.

Channel fever—expectation one feels when homeward bound.

Crutches—slang for booms designed to tow nets and depressors to dampen a vessel's roll.

Depressor—Weighted, winged kite-like objects that resist being lifted when submerged in water. Used to dampen vessel roll. Also known as "birds."

Doghouse—enclosure around a door that deflects spray.

Dragger—vessel employing an otter trawl manned by "shovel fishermen."

Dredge—steel frame and bag dragged to harvest scallops.

Eastern rig—vessel with the pilothouse aft of midships.

Faking box—container with removable dowels around the perimeter about which the breeches buoy messenger line is coiled in preparation for use.

Fathom—six feet.

Forecastle—crew quarters forward of the fish hold.

Gallows—A frame with a block at the apex for towing dredges and otter trawls.

Gill net—light netting designed to admit a fish's head securing it behind the gill plates.

Hyflyer—Canadian slang for a buoy with a flag, later with a radar reflector.

Kink—slang for a power nap.

Lanyard—length of line used to control an object or operation.

Line—rope.

Line, branch—one of many short lines attached to a common mainline.

Line, long—line that fishes a few to many thousands of hooks at the same time.

Line, spring—mooring line leading to the dock at opposite end of the vessel.

Loom—halo of a light reflected on the atmosphere above the horizon.

Loran—a system of electronic long-range naviagation.

Lyle gun—small cannon used to deliver a messenger line.

Messenger—strong light line used to deliver a heavier line.

Moon cusser—wrecker (salvager) whose business improves on dark nights.

Navigable semicircle—half of a storm's circulation where its forward progress does not contribute to the local wind speed.

Near sighted—slang for a vessel with the pilothouse forward (Western rig).

Novies—slang for a Nova Scotian, particularly a lobstering-sized boat.

Nun—a cylindrical red navigation buoy with a conical top.

Otter trawl—a conical net held open horizontally with otter boards.

Otter boards—surfaces of wood or steel bridled to tow obliquely causing them to shear away from the direction towed resulting in a wide net mouth opening

Outriggers—reinforced steel booms designed to tow nets and depressors.

Peg—the needle stops on the side of an instrument dial.

Polyball—vinyl plastic inflatable flotation ball with a built-in eye.

Projectile—unarmed cylindrical weight used to deliver messengers.

Quid—plug of tobacco.

Railroller—revolving cylinder mounted on the rail that reduces line friction.

Ripper—a six-inch knife used to gut goundfish.

Scuppers—ports along the rails that allow water overboard.

Shell stock—unshucked bivalves.

Skate the faces—slang for surfing down the face of a following sea.

Slaughterhouse—space in fishhold directly beneath the hatch.

Slurry—one or more solids mixed in a liquid.

Stemming—steering in a direction that negates the effects of wind and tide.

Tinkers—small mackerel also known as spikes.

Triadic stay—wire rope connecting two masts for support of masts and hoisting blocks.

Waist—main deck in the middle of the vessel.

Walk over—when a strong radio signal drowns out a weaker one.

Whale back—rounded shelter over the foredeck.

Western rig—vessel with the wheelhouse forward of midships.

Xiphias gladius—Swordfish, Broadbill.

Illustration Credits

iii Walter H. Rich
2 Maggie Bartlett
3 Rachel Brown
12 Maggie Bartlett
15 Unknown
30 Unknown
34 Walter H. Rich
40 Walter H. Rich
47 Walter H. Rich
48 Walter H Rich
49 Walter H. Rich
55 Walter H. Rich
59 Lutken's "Spolia Atlantica"
61 Curvier & Valencienne, *Histoire Naturelle des Poissons*
134 Ronald K. Stires
138 Walter H. Rich

Others the work of the author

MARTIN BARTLETT served on lifeboat stations, ice breakers, and port security in the Coast Guard during the 1950s. He ran boats and tagged hundreds of tuna with the Woods Hole Oceanographic Institution while promoting and documenting the U.S. east coast longline fishery for swordfish. Later, with the National Marine Fisheries Service and University of Georgia, he engaged in exploratory fishing and gear research resulting in the fishery for swordfish in the Gulf of Mexico.

For the next twenty years as owner/operator of the longliner *Penobscot Gulf*, he fished from Nova Scotia to Texas opening up the swordfishery between Florida and Cape Hatteras. He fished the food chain from swordfish, and tuna down to dogfish and skate wings before taking the *Penobscot Gulf* to the Gulf of Mexico for a short career of sponging.

His articles have appeared in *On the Water*, *Spritsail*, *National Fisherman*, *Commercial Fishing News*, *Commercial Fisheries Review*, and several scientific journals.

Bartlett has "retired" to fresh water in midcoast Maine, running a summer camp for a dozen grandchildren and keeping an eye out for the dorsal wake of an unlucky trophy brown trout.

Made in the USA
Lexington, KY
20 February 2014